*A...
m
to you! Steve Dandy*

Nights of Horseplay

Equine Fantasies from South Carolina's Thoroughbred Country

THE AIKEN SCRIBBLERS GROUP

Gallopalooza

BLS Aiken, LLC

P. O. Box 473

Aiken, SC 29802-0473

BLS Aiken, LLC

A Learning Enterprise

ACKNOWLEDGEMENTS

Map of The Hitchcock Woods used by permission of Steve Black, The Screenprint Factory, Aiken, SC

Photograph of **History Maker** used by permission of The Green Boundary Club, Aiken, SC

Photograph of Painted Horse (**Gallopalooza**) by the Student Art League of the Hite Art Institute at the University of Louisville

Photograph of **Down by the Water** used by permission of University of South Carolina Aiken

Photograph of **Regions Spirit of Aiken** used by permission of Regions Bank, Aiken, SC

Photographs of **William Aiken Sr.** and **Dustin Hoofman** used by permission of URS Corporation, Aiken, SC

Photograph of **His Spirit is the Wind of Aiken** used by permission of Laissez Faire Sotheby's Real Estate, Aiken, SC

Photograph of **Steed Freedom** used by permission of Bank of America, Aiken, SC

Photograph of **Palmetto/American Equine** used by permission of City of Aiken, SC

Editing by Kathy Huff, publisher of *Bella* magazine, Aiken, SC

PREFACE

My first encounter with Aiken was in 1962. On a warm summer evening, my family drove down U.S. 1 en route from Columbia to Augusta. As we rolled down wide tree-lined streets, the thought came to mind: "There is something really special about this place."

My next look came when I went to work at the Savannah River Plant (as it was then known) in 1988. On another warm summer evening, I drove down Whiskey Road in search of a place to dine. Passing Hopelands Gardens and The Green Boundary Club, my old thought came back to me. It was to take many years of living and working here to develop a fuller appreciation of what was special about living in Aiken.

Before Aiken became known as a center of science and technology, it was famous for its horses. A few years ago, a project called "Horseplay" commissioned the creation of thirty-one equine statues. Collectively, they form a picture of Aiken's horse culture over the last century. While many of these statues have moved on to other homes, wherever they are, they serve as ambassadors of the spirit of Aiken.

The Aiken Scribblers is a group of writers in the Aiken – Augusta area who have undertaken this project to celebrate our community and its love of horses. To our local readers, we say, "Enjoy our celebration. You know what it means to live in such a special place." To those readers who have never visited Aiken or who live elsewhere, we say, "Come on by! Our hospitality is always on display. But don't be surprised if you want to settle here permanently."

We dedicate this collection of stories and poems to all those who have made Aiken a place we're proud to call home.

Steve Gordy

TABLE OF CONTENTS

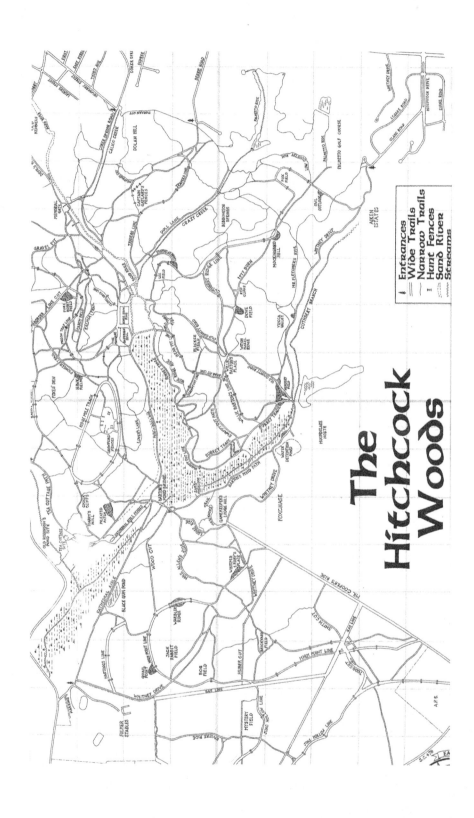

The Hitchcock Woods

Legend:
- ↓ Entrances
- ══ Wide Trails
- ── Narrow Trails
- ├ Hunt Fences
- ╌╌ Sand River
- ~~~ Streams

Exit, Stage Left

Amy Blunt and Will Jones

With 1930s vintage street lamps casting an inviting glow, Newberry Street hardly seemed like the kind of place for a kidnapping.

"Ya g-g-gotta come with us, Jonathon."

Bound and gagged, the hostage struggled, but his protests went unheard outside the deserted Aiken Playhouse. His sneakers skidded along the asphalt as his captor advanced to the waiting car.

A thin, dark-haired man graying at the temples rushed from the back door of the theater and spat in a bad British accent, "Shut up, Reggie." He looked down the street then back the other way before adding, "Are you quite sure the coast is clear? Did you check?"

The big man cowered even as his iron-like grip tightened on the arm of their captive. "Yeah, B-b-boss, I checked. No one's around this time a n-n-night."

"All right then. Hurry and get him into the car."

A muffled expletive sounded from beneath the hood that covered Jonathon's head when Reggie shoved him into the backseat of the Nova.

"Where are we gonna t-t-take him, M-M-Mic—"

"Creele. Remember, Reggie, tonight I'm Creele."

Reggie slid into the passenger seat and smiled his lopsided grin. "Right. Where are we gonna t-t-take him, C-C-Creele."

"The Woods." Creele slammed his door shut with an exasperated sigh. "Don't you listen to anything I say?" The car squealed in reverse, then Creele gunned the motor and sped down Newberry.

Silence settled back over the street and for a moment, the night stilled. Nothing moved, not even a whisper of a breeze in the treetops. The water spouting from the fountain hung suspended in air. The world held its breath until the midnight chimes sounded from St. John's steeple.

At the last chime, William Aiken's hand closed around his pocket watch. The statue of the town's namesake rose from his bench and stretched his bronze arms. From near the entrance to the playhouse, Dustin Hoofman raised his head and shook the length of his body, nose to tail, nearly losing his top hat in the effort. "Mr. Aiken, did you hear that?"

Another horse statue, covered with colorful, equine aphorisms, trotted down Newberry to the playhouse calling, "I did! I did!"

2

"I heard them too, Wordy." Aiken turned to see the horses now standing together at the fountain. "It sounded like a kidnapping to me."

"Serves him right, that prima donna," Wordy said. "It's always all about him. Always has to be his way. Always—"

"That's not true." Dustin stomped his hoof and snorted. "He's a huge star of the stage and screen. A true artist and only wants—"

"Boys," Aiken interrupted. "All that matters now is that he's in trouble and we must aid him. I think we'll need more help. Wordy, you get Spirit from over on Laurens. He knows Hitchcock Woods better than the Aiken Hounds. Dustin, you round up Patriot; he'll know what to do. Last I heard, he's still at Park and Laurens."

As the horses galloped in opposite directions, the bronze watch ticked away their magical moments.

"Reggie, take the brat on the other four-wheeler and follow me."

Jonathon struggled as Reggie helped him mount the bike. "C-c-come on now, Jonathon. D-d-don't make me hurt you. This'll be fun. Have ya ever ridden a f-f-four- wheeler?"

"Shut up!" Creele screeched and sprayed sand up behind him as he headed down the lane toward Memorial Gate. Once past the Gate, they continued down Pete Bostwick trail to the open area of the Show Grounds then took a right and headed up the hill. Through the night they rode, drowning out the crickets' nocturnal serenades.

"Here," Creele called back to Reggie as he turned down a side trail. After busting through the overgrowth, they came to a small clearing and stopped. "Tie him to that tree." Creele pointed, then slithered out of the bag he'd worn on his back.

Reggie pulled the unwilling teenager from the four-wheeler and dragged him to a large pine tree at the edge of the area. He looked anxiously from Creele to Jonathon and back to Creele again.

Creele threw the back pack at him. "There's rope in there."

Reggie caught the bag in one hand, placed his other hand on Jonathon's shoulder, pushing downward until he sat with an "Umph." Three loops later, Jonathon and the pine were tightly united. Reggie dropped the bag at Creele's feet, and flopped down on the four-wheeler, the springs protesting. "What if he has to p-p-pee?"

Creele pinched the giant's man's ear and leaned down to within inches of his face. "How many times do I have to tell you – shut up! Every time you speak, you give him a better chance of identifying us. And if he has to pee, then pee he may - in his trousers. We'll have our ransom within a day. Trust me."

Reggie recoiled as Creele's sour whisper poured into his upturned face. His eyes crossed, and he felt sure his ear would tear off as he leaned away from the stench.

"Now get over there and keep an eye on the brat. I must finalize a few arrangements in town, and will return shortly. Keep your mouth shut and your eyes open. Understand?"

"OK." Reggie's eyes watered. His throat felt tight, as if he'd swallowed a dry walnut.

Dustin and Wordy, now joined by Patriot and Spirit, galloped down South Boundary past the Museum to the narrow road which led into Hitchcock Woods. At the Woods' entrance, they found a parked car.

"Is this their vehicle?" Patriot asked.

"Yeah, that's it," Wordy said. "That's the one. I heard them drive that nag of a horseless carriage all the way down Newberry Street. Then, they—"

"Got it, Wordy. Thanks for the intel." Patriot looked to Spirit. "Looks like they may have taken ATVs from here. Do you see the tracks?"

Spirit of Aiken shook his mane and snorted his disgust. "Four-wheelers in the Woods. Do they have no respect?"

"They're theater people," Dustin defended, "from out of town. They don't know any better."

"Stupid theater people," Wordy started on another roll. "Always on their artistic high horses. Always so excited to see Dustin at the theater entrance. They never walk down the street to appreciate my literary adages. They're probably too—"

"Wordy," Patriot warned, swishing his tail. "Enough. We need to find the hostage. Focus."

"Come on, guys." Spirit trotted down the well-worn path toward Memorial Gate. "I found the tracks."

The horses galloped down Devil's Backbone, pausing only when they'd reached the Show Grounds. The tire tracks crisscrossed, circled over one another, then headed off in opposite directions only to join back up just beyond the schooling jumps in The Manage. The tracks headed up the hill on Pigeon Trap Loop and the horses cantered along beside them.

"Blasted iron horses," Wordy muttered under his breath. "And in the Woods. Unbelievable. Spirit's gonna kick their—"

"Whoa, everybody. Look at this." Spirit nosed the sand where the four-wheeler ruts ended abruptly. The horses halted and scanned the area, noses lifted, but only the screech owls trilled their presence.

"They've covered their tracks," Patriot said in a low nicker. "They must be near."

"Here." Spirit turned down a small, overgrown trail fifty feet away. "Shhh."

The horses maneuvered silently down the steep trail into the woods. Soon the undergrowth began to thin, and they could see a clearing up ahead. In the moonlight, they could clearly see the teen and a large man.

Against the tree, Jonathon began to squirm, but when his movements became more violent, like epileptic spasms, Reggie jumped to his feet and ran to untie him. The squeals behind the duct tape grew into sustained, muffled screams as Reggie struggled with the knots.

At last, the ropes gave way and Reggie helped Jonathon up, but Jonathon continued to stamp his feet and shake. Reggie removed the hood, peeled off the duct tape and sealed Jonathon's mouth with his coconut-sized palm.

"Y-y-you have to be quiet." Reggie looked down into terrified eyes. "Y-y-you have to tell me what's wrong."

Jonathon nodded rapidly. Reggie loosened his grip.

"Something's biting me."

"C-c-come away from that tree." Reggie guided Jonathon a few steps from the tree and helped to brush the ants from Jonathon's body.

"I-I-I'm sorry. I m-m-must have sat you down on a fire ant m-m-mound. I'm s-s-sorry. "

"I think they're all off now," Jonathon said, looking into Reggie's face for the first time. "That was like a horror movie. Like I was being burned alive. What did you call them?

"Fire ants," Reggie said.

"Fire ants," Patriot whispered in unison from deeper in the woods.

"Those are the worst!" Dustin hissed.

"I'm so sorry. B-b-but in the dark I couldn't tell they were there. A-a-and Mr. Creele was in a—" Reggie stopped abruptly, his eyes widening.

"What?"

"I t-t-took your hood off."

"It doesn't matter. I know who you are. Both of you."

"B-b-but he said as long as you didn't see us, you couldn't identify us. W-w-we would split the money, and you would be back with the group in a couple days. He knows they can get the money f-f-fast. As long as you don't know who we are, we c-c-can't be identified."

"He works with the troupe. How could I not know his voice, especially that pretentious English accent? And you're one of the set people. It's hard to miss that stutter."

"I d-d-do st-st-stutter. Mr. Creele s-s-said he would t-t-take me to a therapist with the m-m-money, so I could t-t-take acting l-l-lessons."

"*You* want to act?" Jonathon stared at Reggie in disbelief but quickly shifted his tone. "Well, it would be difficult, but you could overcome stuttering just like King George VI."

Reggie blushed, going a faint purple in the moonlight. "Y-y-you're just being kind."

"*Kind*? You've seen me criticize the others during rehearsals, Reggie. Is *kind* my style?"

"No. You're m-m-mean."

"I'm not mean. Demanding, yes. Direct, absolutely. I always give my best effort and require the same from everyone else in the troupe." Jonathon studied Reggie for a moment. "I've never spoken to you, have I?"

"N-n-no. You think I'm just a carpenter, n-n-not worth talking to."

Wordy swatted Dustin with his tail. "See, I told you he's a prima donna. Too good to talk to the stage hands. All that fame's gone to his head—"

"Shhh," Patriot whispered.

"Wrong." Jonathon checked the ground before settling beside Reggie. "I see your work every day. It's quality work. I haven't spoken to you because you get it."

"R-r-really?"

"Is *lying* my style?"

Reggie burst into laughter. "At the b-b-backstage party in New York, after he mis-quoted Shakespeare, you told Mayor B-B-Bloomberg he was a pompous m-m-meg—"

"A megalomaniac with no knowledge of theater. Yeah, I remember. Probably not one of my better moments," Jonathon said with a sheepish grin.

"B-b-but true," Reggie laughed again and Jonathon joined him.

Above their merriment, the whine of an ATV grew progressively louder in the night. Reggie and Jonathon stopped mid-chuckle and stared wide-eyed at each other.

"Creele!" exclaimed everyone, including the horses still hidden in the forest.

If he had been a cartoon character, steam would have been billowing out of Creele's ears as he parked the ATV and stomped across the clearing. Reggie stepped in front of Jonathon before Creele reached them.

"F-f-fire ants," Reggie shouted though Creele was only a few feet away. "I c-c-couldn't let him get eaten up."

"Tie him back up, you blithering idiot. My instructions were that you not remove the hood for any reason."

"It's over, Creele," Jonathon said, coming around from behind his protector.

Creele's dark eyes bored into Jonathon's. His thin lips twisted into a wry smile. "It will indeed be over soon."

Patriot watched the silver barrel emerge from Creele's pocket. The pistol glinted in the moonlight. "He's got a gun."

"Oh my God! Is it a Colt .45?" Wordy exclaimed.

The other three horses stared at him.

"Well, is it?" Wordy whispered.

"From here, it looks like a small caliber, semi-automatic, a cheap Saturday Night Special," Patriot said.

"W-w-why do you have a g-g-gun, Creele?"

"I told you to tie him up."

"B-b-but he's not going to run. He —"

Creele pointed the gun directly between Jonathon's eyes. "Now!"

"O-O-OK."

"Tape his trap shut, put the hood back on him, and tie him onto the four-wheeler."

With a shorter length of rope from Creele's backpack, Reggie loosely bound Jonathon to the console of the ATV and whispered, "Hold on as b-b-best you c-c-can. We've got to make a b-b-break for it. I g-g-gotta g-g-get you outta here."

"He'll never let us out of the woods," Jonathon whispered.

Creele jerked the keys from the other vehicle's ignition then came closer to his hostage. "Good, Reggie. Now step away from him."

Reggie didn't move.

"Step away!" Creele screeched and waved the gun at Reggie until the giant stumbled back a few yards.

"Get ready, boys" Patriot said, muscles tensed.

Jumping on the ATV behind Jonathon, Creele gunned the engine to life.

"B-b-but wait!" Reggie lunged forward.

Patriot charged. "Now!" All four horses burst into the clearing just as the gunshot cracked the night air. Reggie's pained howl drowned out Creele's surprised oaths hurled at the intruders, but by the time Reggie dropped to the pine straw, Creele was already zooming up the overgrown trail.

"He's getting away! We should chase him! We can catch him!" Wordy pranced in place at the edge of the trail leading out.

Spirit nosed the still figure on the ground.

"Is he dead?" Dustin snuffled Reggie's hair. "Oh, please don't be dead."

"Wordy, get over here," Patriot ordered.

"What? Who?" Reggie's eyes opened and widened in a single movement.

"It's all right, Reggie," Spirit reassured. "We're here to help."

"Oh, thank the Lord!" Dustin said, falling to his knees.

"Dustin, you and Wordy help Reggie. Spirit and I are going to track Creele. Meet us at the crossing as soon as Reggie is able to ride."

"Ride?" Wordy, Dustin, and Reggie repeated together.

"B-b-but you're, umm, s-s-statues?"

"They'll explain on the way." In a flash of moonlight, Patriot and Spirit were gone.

"Not to worry, Sir Reginald," Dustin bowed to him. "Wordy is a brave warhorse and would be honored to carry a wounded soldier—"

"ME? What about you? You carry him. He's too big for me," said Wordy

"Wordy." Dustin stomped a hoof. "We're the same model."

"C-c-can one of you carry me cuz C-C-Creele's getting away with Jonathon?"

"This way."

Instead of returning the way they'd come, Spirit turned north toward Rabbit Valley. Soon the horses caught sight of the four-wheeler and galloped on. When they got close though, Creele turned, firing wildly in their general direction. The horses dropped back to a safer distance as Creele raced over the

Ridge Mile Track before heading back down the steep trail to The Manage.

"I don't think he knows he's going in a giant circle," Spirit said as he and Patriot jumped a fence abreast.

"Well, I guess he might be a little distracted, being chased by inanimate objects and all." The horses snickered. "You remember the plan?"

"Past the Show Grounds to the crossing," Spirit recited.

Patriot nodded and took off in a dead run.

Spirit winced as Patriot raced past Creele through the perfectly manicured grass of the Show Grounds, tearing up the turf reserved for one special show every spring. Once Patriot had a good head start, Spirit lowered his head and raced up behind the ATV, herding it down Pete Bostwick's trail, directly toward Patriot waiting in the dark.

"Come on, Reggie. You can do it," Dustin cheered.

Reggie tried to struggle onto Wordy's slippery back while holding the sleeve of his blood-soaked shirt. "I c-c-can't do this."

"Here." Dustin trotted over with the rope that Reggie had used to tie Jonathon to the tree. "Wrap this around Wordy's neck so you have something to hold on to."

Reggie stared at the theater horse for a moment. "Y-y-you're smart for a s-s-statue."

Dustin sniffed. "Thank you. I can recite *Richard III* entirely from memory, you know. *Now is the winter of our discontent....*"

Wordy rolled his eyes.

Spirit bore down on the four-wheeler and was two lengths behind when Patriot burst from the trees, running straight at the vehicle. Instinctively, Creele veered hard to the right to avoid the mass coming at him and plunged headlong into what appeared to be a riverbed filled with sand.

"What the…?" Creele scrambled from the ATV as it slowly began to sink but as soon as he stood, the sand began to suck him down too. The harder he tried to escape, the faster he sank.

Muffled shouts coming from the sinking four-wheeler brought the horses' attention back to its bound captive.

"I'll go after him," Patriot said.

Spirit shook his mane. "No, you'll get caught in the mire too."

"We've got to get him out of there." Patriot paced the along the bank.

"Hey, what about me?" Creele flailed in the quicksand, still eight feet from the bank.

"Untie Jonathon and we'll consider helping you out," Patriot said.

Creele looked at Patriot and back at the four-wheeler. He'd already made it half way to the shore. "No, I'm not going back there. We'll both die."

"Suit yourself." Patriot shrugged and trotted away from him.

"Wait!" Creele cried. "Wait, I'll untie him. Of course, I will." Creele struggled back toward Jonathon as muffled cries sounded from beneath the hood.

"Do you hear that?" Spirit lifted his nose to the air then spun in a circle. A second later, hoofbeats thudded in the night.

"Dustin, over here," Patriot called.

"We've got Reggie!" Dustin shouted.

"WE?" Wordy puffed and slowed to a trot his sides heaving.

"J-J-Jonathon," Reggie bellowed. A muffled cry answered him.

"I'm trying to save him," Creele huffed, "but I can't get through this muck." Waist deep, Creele was trapped too.

"We have to get to him. He's tied onto that thing," Reggie said, slipping from Wordy's back.

Wordy looked at Dustin. "Did you notice? Not even a hint of a stutter."

Reggie rushed to the bank. "Hang on, Jonathon, I'm coming!"

"Stop!" Patriot shouted to Reggie who slid to a halt. "Use the rope from Wordy's neck."

"But he's tied. He can't grab it."

"Take one end and once you've got him untied, we'll pull you both in."

"Hey, how about me? You could pull me in first."

But no one bothered to answer Creele's pleas as Reggie unwound the rope from Wordy's neck and plunged into the sand. By the time he reached Jonathon, the drag had him at the knees.

"Hurry," Jonathon cried, once free of the tape and hood. Tears streamed down his face.

"I'm gonna get you outta here." Reggie worked blindly at the swollen knots of the ropes already submerged below the surface of the sand.

Dustin paced the edge of the river reciting Shakespeare. *"A horse! A horse! My kingdom for a horse…"*

"Hurry," Patriot said.

Spirit muttered a low prayer.

"I didn't carry that very *large* person," Wordy began, "all the way across Hitchcock Woods to save Jonathon, only for them both to drown in quicksand. Really, how would this look as a new addition to my graffiti – 'failed hero' or 'the horse that couldn't' or—"

"Got it!" Reggie shouted.

"Great, now both of you hang on to the rope and I'll pull you out." Patriot grabbed the other end between his teeth and began to back up. The rope went taut and he gave a backwards heave but nothing happened. The quicksand held them fast.

"Lay out flat," Spirit said, then grabbed the rope in his teeth. Wordy and Dustin were quick to follow suit. With all four horses pulling, Reggie and Jonathon inched closer to the shore.

"Hey, don't forget me over here!" Creele shouted, now chest-deep in the sand.

Once on the bank, Jonathon stared wide-eyed at the living horse statues. "They're…they're alive."

"These are our friends," Reggie explained as he pointed to each horse. "Spirit, Patriot, Dustin, and my warhorse – Wordy."

Wordy looked over at Dustin and sniffed.

It was Jonathon's turn to stutter. "B-b-but how—"

"There's no time for that now," Patriot said. "Wordy, Dustin – you need to get these two back to town. We're almost out of time."

"Back to town? I don't know which way town is," Dustin looked at Wordy, who snorted and shook his head.

"Spirit, take them back. The shortest route possible," Patriot instructed.

"What about him?" Spirit nodded to Creele.

"I'll take care of him," Patriot said watching Creele as he tried to tread water in the sand. "Now go on while there's still time."

Using a nearby fallen tree to mount, soon Reggie and Jonathon sat astride Wordy and Dustin. Spirit eyed his brave friend a moment longer before galloping down the trail, calling for the others to follow.

"Well, now isn't this an interesting turn of events," Patriot said, pacing back and forth along the bank.

"Please," Creele begged, "please pull me out. I promise I'll never do anything like this again. I just wanted to go to England and see real Shakespearean theater. I didn't want to hurt anyone—"

"Silence," Patriot commanded. The statue covered with scenes of American bravery eyed the pitiful creature slowly sinking to his demise. After another long moment, Patriot picked up the rope they'd used to pull the others out. Placing a hoof over one end he picked the other end up in his teeth and flung it to Creele.

Struggling against the sand, Creele managed to free an arm and grasp the knotted end which had neatly landed inches from his face. His other arm came free from the suck with a pop and he held the rope like a life line, which indeed it was.

"Got it. Now pull!" His urgent request came out like an order, and Patriot stood watching him as the precious seconds ticked by.

"If there is any chance of your rescue, we must both pull," Patriot said.

"Yes, yes, of course," Creele said with a note of near repentance.

And pull they did. Patriot leaned back, the muscles in his haunches straining. Creele pulled himself forward along the rope a millimeter at a time.

"I...I think it's working," Creele gasped.

The snare of hoofbeats upon brick announced their arrival as Spirit, Dustin with Jonathon, and Wordy, carrying a slumped Reggie, arrived at William Aiken's bench. With a screech of metal, Aiken sprang to his feet to help Reggie slide from Wordy's back. Jonathon and Aiken eased Reggie's enormous frame to the ground beside the fountain wall.

"He's going into shock," Aiken said. "Stay with him; someone will come along soon."

"Dustin, Wordy, back to your places. Time's up." Aiken sat and assumed his statue pose.

Jonathon collapsed beside Reggie and said, "Thanks for … for everything. Wordy, they should rename you Bucephalus."

"Bu-what?"

Dustin shouldered Wordy. "The curtain is closing, my loquacious friend. Time for us to exit, stage left. Until next time."

As Dustin and Wordy galloped toward their stands, Wordy asked, "Bu-who?"

"Bucephalus," Aiken said. "You know, one of the most famous horses in history. Alexander the Great's warhorse."

"I am Bucephalus the Great," Wordy whinnied as he mounted his platform.

"I can't get back in time to take my place," Spirit nickered to Aiken. "I'll remain here with you. No doubt they'll believe USCA students have been playing tricks again." Spirit straightened into his well-practiced pose and became still as a statue as the morning's first light began to brighten Newberry Street.

"Well, what have we here?" a blue uniform spoke to Jonathon who slept propped up against the fountain wall. "A couple of vandals too partied-out to leave the scene of the crime?"

"I'm not so sure about that, Carlos," said a second uniform. "This one's been shot."

A thin mist, drifting just above the ground, softened the world around the three early morning riders. Towering pines and regal magnolias stood guard above the girls as they trotted down Pete Bostwick Trail.

"Wow, check this out." Coleen reined in the quick-stepping mare to wait for her friends, who trailed a few strides behind.

The three horses snorted and spooked while the girls stared in disbelief.

"I've never seen anything like it," Liza said.

"Who put this out here?" Tina asked.

"Maybe it's some sort of modern art project," Colleen said.

"Maybe," Tina agreed. "It's certainly a good way to warn people about the quicksand."

"I bet someone from the Center for the Arts commissioned it," Liza said. "It's really well done. Look how life-like the guy looks, like he's trying with all his might to pull himself out."

"I'm glad they made it a *man* being pulled out by the horse and not a woman," Tina said. "Much more believable. A woman would have just read the sign." Tina pointed to the wooden board nailed to a tree a dozen feet down the bank which clearly stated "Danger - Quicksand."

The girls continued on past the statues, their laughter filling the dewy morning air.

William Aiken Sr.

Introducing Miss Evelyn

Lisa Wright-Dixon

Evelyn always wanted to be an actress. She hadn't told anyone about her dream because she was from a practical family. According to her mother, being an actress was not practical. Evelyn's mother wanted her to have a career that would consistently pay the rent, put food in her belly, and clothes on her back. Therefore, acting was out. Evelyn asked her mother for a practical career choice for a girl of nine to pursue.

"Well," her mother said, "Why not be a nurse? You could even be a doctor. It's good for women to set their goals high." But just like every other career suggestion, something would happen to ruin it for Evelyn. The day she cut her finger and passed out over a drop of blood, she realized the doctor dream was out.

Evelyn always returned to make believe. In her child's mind, she could go anywhere, be anything, and see anyone she wanted. She traveled abroad to the continents in her fantasy world. She met William and Kate, the Duke and Duchess, and even had afternoon tea with his grandmother, the Queen, at Windsor. She frequently visited Robert Pattinson and Kristen Stewart who played Edward and Bella in the "Twilight" saga. They were her absolute favorite characters. There were many adventures in front of Evelyn's bedroom mirror. Everything in her imagination was possible, even a great acting career.

Evelyn lived in a small community in South Carolina named Aiken. On occasion, Evelyn's mother would take her to see a play at the town's community theater. Evelyn cherished these moments. Whatever play she saw, that night, she would go home and imagine herself in it as the lead character. One night, after seeing "Romeo and Juliet," Evelyn took stage in front of her bedroom mirror in the lead role of Juliet. Evelyn's brother, who was prone to spying and other acts of despicable destitution, snuck up on her and watched her performance.

"Romeo, Romeo, wherefore art thou, Romeo?" Evelyn imagined her Romeo, Robert Pattinson, gazing into her eyes.

"Oh, Romeo, you can kiss my pursed lips, or sink thou glorious fangs into the veins of my neck!" Evelyn exaggerated, offering her neck to an imaginary Edward Cullen.

"Darling Edward, I mean, Romeo," Evelyn fumbled her line. "Won't you take me as your Bella, I mean, as your Juliet?" Evelyn heard a commotion at her bedroom door. She spun around to her snickering brother, who was rolling on the floor in a fit of laughter.

"You evil troll," Evelyn said it with passion and conviction. "I'm telling Mom!"

"I'm telling Mom, I'm telling Mom," he provokingly mimicked. Evelyn's brother was twelve and always had a discouraging word for her.

"You can't act you weirdo," he said as spitefully as he could. "Besides, Dumbo, Romeo isn't a vampire." Her brother was evil incarnate.

"What do you know about it?" Evelyn was annoyed that he wasn't intelligent enough to see the parallel between Romeo and Juliet and Edward and Bella, the couple from the "Twilight" saga. "I'm an actress and I can make up whatever I want." Evelyn felt the need to justify her story.

"YOU'RE an actress?" He ridiculed mockingly. "You can't be an actress, Mom won't let you!"

"Yes I can, if I want. I can pretend I'm anything." Evelyn felt tears starting to sting her eyes, mostly because she knew he was right. Her mother wouldn't stand for this impractical nonsense.

"I'm telling Mom," he yelled over his shoulder as he bounded down the stairs to their living room. Evelyn sighed. Although her mother would scold her for being silly, Evelyn felt she would be scolded for having dreams. Evelyn knew she had the ability to evoke emotion from people with her stories. Already, she could captivate them with her antics. And even though she loved her mother dearly and didn't want to disappoint her, she knew she couldn't do anything else but act. Her imagination was endless and she knew that had to account for something worthwhile. Evelyn saw clearly what she had to do. She would need to prove herself to her mother and brother. Evelyn decided to run away to become a great actress.

The next day was Saturday. Evelyn awoke to the tantalizing aroma of pancakes and bacon drifting through the house. Not to be detoured, she began packing her belongings. She packed light, taking what little would fit in her Twilight backpack.

She grabbed her savings hidden under her bed in a mason jar. She sat her backpack upright and zipped it looking directly at Bella Swan, who was euphoric and protected in Edward's embrace.

"Here goes, Bells," Evelyn sighed. "I hope I know what I'm doing." With one final look around her room, Evelyn headed toward the bedroom door. Suddenly, she saw her brother scurrying down the hallway. If he told her mother, the plan would be ruined! Evelyn made a quick decision. She would have to leave now.

Evelyn tiptoed to the bottom of the stairs. Peering around the corner, she saw her brother shoveling pancakes into his mouth. The smell of food was powerful. It made Evelyn weak. It was probably not a good decision to leave on an empty stomach, but she didn't want to take the chance of being stopped. Her mother's back was turned. Evelyn quickly shot to the back door.

"Where are you going young lady?" It was impossible. Evelyn couldn't even fathom how her mother could see out of the back of her head.

"I thought I'd get an early start," stuttered Evelyn. "Going to Claire's house today to, uh, hang out." It wasn't a complete lie. She had planned on going past her friend Claire's house on her way to town. Evelyn's mother eyed her backpack.

"What's in there?" She asked in a motherly, suspicious, accusatory way, all at the same time.

"Twilight stupid stuff," her brother goaded. He made mockery of all things Twilight and sacred. Thankfully, he had only seen her put Twilight DVDs in the backpack during his spying. After all, she couldn't leave those behind, they were a prized possession.

"Shut up, you ... "

"Don't be rude to your brother. Sit down and eat first." Evelyn obeyed the command. All was well. Nothing had been revealed. After eating enough for three meals, Evelyn kissed her mother goodbye and headed out to claim her destiny.

It took an hour for Evelyn to walk from her house to the Aiken Community Theater. She figured her trek should start from a place of meaning in the acting world. Evelyn loved the horse statues around Aiken. She especially loved the one outside the theater. His name was Dustin Hoofman. He had a top hat, tuxedo, and a walking stick, just like Fred Astaire. Mr. Astaire had once owned a home in Aiken. It was even said that the actor danced down the steps of the Old Post Office on Laurens Street, a sight Evelyn wished she could have seen.

Whenever Evelyn came to see a show, she would speak to Mr. Hoofman and pet his cheek. Evelyn thought he had class and style, and she told her mother so right in front of him. Evelyn imagined Mr. Hoofman would of course want her to call him by his first name. She figured Dustin knew everyone in the acting community, as well as in Hollywood. He would be a great friend to have in her corner along the way. Evelyn put her hand on Dustin's back. She leaned down to whisper in his ear.

"Wish me luck ... I'll be gone for awhile, I'll miss you." Evelyn stood up. She stepped back in horror at what she saw. It was her brother and his two crummy friends that liked to tease her relentlessly.

"Surprise, Dumbo!" He sounded more cruel than usual.

"Are you talking to that statue?" He didn't wait for an answer.

"I knew you were up to something, so me and the guys thought we'd follow you."

"Go away! You shouldn't have followed me," Evelyn screamed.

"Hey guys, my sister is running away to become an actress." He said it with much disdain. The other two, Evelyn referred to them as Duffo and Duffet, chimed in with abuse.

"That's the stupidest thing I ever heard" Duffo looked at Duffet, giving him the cue to speak.

"Yeah," said Duffet, "stupidest ever." Evelyn turned to walk away.

"I'm telling Mom, Dumbo, you won't get far." He was triumphant.

"Go ahead." Evelyn glared defiantly. "I'm still going, you can't stop me." Evelyn started to run. Instinctively, as a lion would chase a gazelle, Evelyn's brother, along with Duffo and Duffet, chased her right into the road in front of an oncoming car. The last thing Evelyn saw was Dustin Hoofman tipping his hat with his cane, bidding her farewell.

"You almost bought the farm." The voice sounded far away. "Can you get up?" Evelyn felt a nudge under her head, neck, and back. She squinted to gain focus.

"Come on now, snap out of it." The voice was more persistent. Evelyn struggled to get to her feet.

"Oh, ow ... " Her head hurt bad. Even though Evelyn could see, she reasoned her vision was not clear, because standing in front of her was Dustin Hoofman ... ALIVE! It was his voice she heard!

"Well, at least you didn't run ... you know, a statue is talking to you. Although, I'm not sure, 'cause I'm a talking statue, not a human, but if I were human, I would think that if a statue started talking to me ... oh, yeah, throw in the fact that the statue is an animal, a horse, which, you know, horses don't talk. I'm just sayin', I feel pretty confident, that I'd run." Evelyn's mouth hung open. He continued on.

"Okay ... this isn't going well ... " The Phenomenon took a step back and circled Evelyn. "Let me try again." He looked pensive. "Me Dustin Hoofman, talking horse statue, me here to help you follow your dream." He was being sarcastic. Not only that, he sounded exactly like Dustin Hoffman, the actor.

Somehow, Evelyn formed her words.

"This is a dream ... horses don't talk," Evelyn tried to be as matter -of- fact as a person in shock could be. He raised his horse eyebrows.

"Technically, how do you know?" He was being a little combative. Evelyn shook her head. She felt indignant. How dare he question her?

"Cause I know, horses don't talk, oh, and wait, statues of horses don't talk." Evelyn knew she was being rude but he deserved his sarcasm right back. Besides, he didn't know her well enough to have an attitude.

"Okay, then, I'm a horse, I'm a statue, I'm talking ... and, if you haven't noticed, I sound exactly like my namesake." He was gloating now. But he did, he really did sound like Dustin Hoffman.

"Then this is a dream, like I said ... so ... am I sleeping in the middle of the day?" Evelyn was just trying to make sense of it all.

"Not exactly … okay, don't get scared, okay? Everything is obviously all right because you're having this crazy dream, right?" He was trying his best to keep her calm.

"Oh no, oh no, oh no…" She felt panicky.

"No no, it's not what you think," he was trying to be reassuring, but it wasn't working.

"I'm dead … I'm dead … I'm nine years old and I'm dead?" Suddenly, Evelyn missed her mother.

"No, oh no, but … you're a bit messed up."

"Messed up? What does that mean?" All she felt was hysteria.

"Okay, you got hit by a car when you ran into the street … you're a little unconscious right now," he said it only the way Dustin Hoffman could.

"So I'm not dead?"

"No, you are not dead."

"Anything broken?" Evelyn poked her ribs.

"No … bruised, not broken." He said it as if it could have been worse.

"I'm okay?" She was starting to believe him.

"You're okay … well …" He lingered on his hesitation.

"Oh no, well what?"

"Well, you are having this nutty dream. You got a good bump on the noggin," he reasoned with a matter -of- fact tilt of his head.

Evelyn looked around. It was nutty, good nutty, imagination nutty.

"I know where I am. I know this place," Evelyn was beaming.

"You're right. It's Hollywood Boulevard, the Walk of Fame." Dustin took his cane and waved it towards the stars on the street as if he were the ringmaster introducing the opening act of his three-ring circus.

"How did you know I was going to say that?"

"I can read your mind. It's a dream, remember?" Evelyn contemplated the dream aspect. "Cool, very cool." She was delighted with the situation. "So, if it's a dream, I can do anything I want?"

"Yes, to a certain point. It's part subconscious, but yes, you can guide your thoughts a bit." He was glad she was easing up.

"Can I make you look a bit hipper?" Evelyn felt a sudden liking for her guide.

"Sure, whatever you like." He was friendly. "It's your dream."

Evelyn imagined Dustin Hoofman as a beautiful thoroughbred. His tuxedo was red with a white tie and white top hat. His walking stick became solid gold.

"Nice touch, kid," referring to his gold cane, Dustin used it to tip his hat.

"What is this dream about?" Evelyn was getting curious.

"It's about you, Evelyn. It's about you and your dreams."

"You mean, THE dream? The one no one says I can do?"

"That would be the one. I am here to tell you that dreams do come true." Dustin bowed when he said this to Evelyn. He looked majestic.

"Thank you, I appreciate that. Don't get me wrong, but why would you be the one chosen to tell me that?"

"Well, you did pat me on the cheek and tell me goodbye. And I do believe I was the last thing you saw before you went unconscious. So, why not me? You like me, right?"

"Oh yes I always have. In fact, I think you are the most stylish of all the statue horses in town. In fact," Evelyn stopped; she was getting too personal and blushed.

"I know," Dustin winked at her. "You want to jump on my back and take a picture … it's okay … everyone wants to sit on us for pictures, but the city won't allow it. You know there's that fine and all." Dustin seemed flattered. "Back to you, Evelyn. I need to tell you not to give up on your dreams. Many times in life you will encounter people who try to distract you from your true calling. They aren't always bad people, in fact, sometimes, they're the people who love us most."

"You mean, like my mother." Evelyn remembered her conversation with her mother the night before. "Why doesn't she believe in me? Why doesn't she see acting is all I want to do?" Evelyn desperately needed to understand.

"Sometimes people are afraid." He sounded contemplative again.

"Afraid of what?"

"Afraid that maybe you'll be hurt. It's not that she doesn't believe in you, Evelyn. It's just that she is afraid for you, afraid that you may struggle, and give up, and be discouraged. She wants to shield you from any thing in this world that will harm you in any way, and that includes pursuing dreams."

"Wow! So, it's not that she thinks I can't do it, she just doesn't want me to be disappointed?" This was a huge revelation.

"That's it, kid, in a subconscious nutshell. You got it."

"I shouldn't run away then, should I?"

"No, that's probably not the best idea. You're nine years old. You don't have a job, you don't have a car. Well, you can't drive, you're nine. Anyway, you left the house and within an hour, you got hit by a car. You may want to rethink this whole situation ... not to mention food. You're getting hungry aren't you?"

"Yeah, whoa, yeah, I am starving." Evelyn stood in front of Dustin. "So what's next?" Evelyn was ready for anything. She felt the weight of the world lift off her shoulders. Dustin proceeded to host her dream.

"Well, you're going to wake up, and you will be in the hospital, and your family, including your brother ... By the way, what is up with him?" Dustin looked at Evelyn with amazed confusion, waiting for an explanation.

"He's just ... different?" For lack of a better description, Evelyn left it at that.

"Well, he will be even more different now but in a good way after all this."

"He will?" Evelyn felt hope.

"Oh yes," Dustin was confident, "he thinks he killed you. The two of you will have a better sister-brother relationship after this." Dustin looked wise. "Everything happens for a reason, Evelyn, always remember that. Everything happens for a reason."

"Will my mother understand better now too? I mean, like I understand her now?"

"Yes, but it will take some work, on both your parts. But things will mend, this I can guarantee." Dustin winked at her again. "Now young lady," he said in a playful tone, before you wake up, we must discuss this matter of Team Edward ... is there any way to convince you to walk on Jacob's side?"

Sweet Brew and a Cherry Cane

Phyllis Maclay

One reason why birds and horses are happy is because they are not trying to impress other birds and horses.

– Dale Carnegie

Eleven horse heads swayed on the flatbed trailer that crawled down the lazy "S" in the road. The shiny, colorful statues flashed reflections of the warm October sun as the equine figures seemed to silently take in their new surroundings of Crooked Creek, a small subdivision just outside Aiken city limits. I didn't know it back then, but that Saturday things were going to be different in our little neighborhood.

Front doors popped open and residents poured out to gather around the truck as it whined to a stop in front of Mr. Elliot's house, the last home on the cul-de-sac. He was already at the end of his driveway, leaning on his cane, with a smile on his face that was contagious. Something about him fascinated me like no other person I knew. Maybe it was the stories he told, like how he came to own his cherry wood cane with horses carved on it. After winning it in a bet with a ringmaster at a circus he visited last year in Texas, it was his constant companion. He hinted that it might have a little magic in it, but of course I didn't believe that part. After all, I had just turned eleven two weeks and five days ago.

I dropped the pink curtain to my upstairs bedroom window and hurried outside with my older sister, Tory, just in time to see Hazel Stone, the neighborhood Nazi of rules and regulations, parting people like Moses divided the Red Sea, to get to the truck.

"Step back! Step back, y'all," yelled Wanda Sidberry who navigated herself to Hazel's side. Wanda was always next to Hazel at these neighborhood gatherings like a magnet on a fridge.

I looked around to see that all of my neighbors were here to help get Mr. Elliot's fiberglass horses off the truck - and I suspect some came to see what he was going to do with them. I had heard the horse statues around Aiken were getting a bit weathered by our hot Carolina sun and recent droughts. The owners didn't know what to do with them so Mr. Elliot bought them all and arranged for their transportation to Crooked Creek.

"Is Mom coming?" I asked Tory. She piled her long dark hair on top of her head and fanned her neck.

"Yeah, she's right behind Gabby and Rico over there, see?"

The Salas couple thought I was waving at them, then laughed when they realized Mom was behind them. They were the newest family to move to Crooked Creek, right next door to us. Their sons, Andy and Sam, weren't anywhere to be seen.

While Sam was an annoying eight-year-old, Andy was becoming one of my best friends. We often walked up and down the road talking, or hung out on the big log that crossed Crooked Creek behind my house.

Russ and Louise Gregory, the first people to move into Crooked Creek, tramped up to the truck. Miss Louise smiled as she adjusted her straw hat.

"Quiet, quiet," shouted Wanda, clapping her hands for us to settle down like she was our Sunday School teacher or something. Melvin, her husband, rolled his eyes. Tory and I giggled.

"The sooner you let me speak, the sooner we can advise Mr. Elliot on the placement of his horses." announced Hazel. "I will read off the names of our Home Owner Association members. Just raise your hand if you are here."

"What should we do if we aren't?" asked Rico. Everyone laughed and thought that was funny, except Hazel and her clone, Wanda.

"Stand silent for the roll call," commanded Wanda as she nodded to Hazel.

"Stand silent? Should we salute?" Tory whispered.

"Next she'll use a bull horn," I whispered back. Tory and I almost busted a gut when Wanda brought her hand from behind her back and handed Hazel ... a yellow bullhorn. She held it to her mouth.

"Please give me your attention."

"Really, Hazel?" hollered Rico while Gabby tried to shush him. "A bullhorn? We're all right here in front of you."

"Some people may be audibly impaired," said Hazel defensively.

"Don't know about that, but that dang thing will make me deaf," snarled Mr. Gregory as his wife patted his arm.

"You're losing control of the crowd," Wanda warned Hazel.

"All right, back to matters at hand, people," Hazel proclaimed. "Mr. Elliot, what do you plan to do with these horses? We have a beautiful neighborhood where everyone has a 150-foot front lawn that is fertilized and dandelion free. Trees and flower beds are allowed as long as they are maintained properly. But I don't know of anything that allows statues out front. What are you going to do with them?"

"Well, Miss Hazel, it's a surprise." Mr. Elliot cocked his head and grinned.

"Surprises are not allowed in this neighborhood," piped in Wanda. "They have to be planned."

Mom laughed. That got a stabbing glance from Hazel.

Mr. Elliot raised his cane. "If all my kind neighbors will help the truck driver get the statues off the truck and just put them in my front yard - for now, Miss Haze- I will be forever grateful and you can all go home."

Before Hazel could find the "on" button to the bullhorn, all the neighbors – except Wanda -- shuffled over like a giant amoeba to unload the statues. The horse I touched felt smooth as I ran my palm over a moon painted on its neck. The statues were arranged in a circle just off the driveway in Mr. Elliot's yard. As the truck groaned away from us, Mr. Elliot watched us mill around, petting and touching the statues. He caught me looking at him, and smiled as his cane tapped the ground. My palm grew warmer as it rested on the statue. Placing it against my cheek, the tapping sound of Mr. Elliot's cane grew louder until it was all I could hear. The warmth on my palm was all I could feel.

Mr. Elliot's smile was all I could see. I was like a sponge soaking it all into my brain until I zoned out.

I felt a finger poking my back and turned to see Andy's dark eyes and grinning face. "Hey, Liza! I just got here. This is pretty cool. What's Mr. E going to do with the horses?"

"He's not saying. You know how he is."

I looked across the street and saw Hazel and Wanda retreating to the Stones' front porch. Bless their hearts.

"May I just have a minute of your time," called out Mr. Elliot. The neighbors fell silent and looked at him as he walked over to the closest statue. "Let me introduce you to your new neighbors." I noticed as he walked by each horse, Mr. E tapped their legs gently with his cherry cane.

Mr. Williams, who lived at the entrance of Crooked Creek, approached Mr. Elliot. "What are you going to do with them? Hazel is right when she says we have a well-designed neighborhood. Any of our front yards could be on the cover of Southern Living. Let's keep it that way. It's good for property appreciation."

"I would never ruin anything beautiful," assured Mr. Elliot. "Now thank y'all and have a good day." He winked at me and walked back to his house. The crowd broke up and Andy invited me to his kitchen for lunch. You don't have to ask this girl twice to come eat homemade tamales and chalupas. Me gusto mucho.

The next Monday a pickup truck full of hired hands chugged into Mr. Elliot's drive as I was leaving for school with my dad. When I came home after soccer practice, Mr. Elliot's horses were lined up on his driveway as if waiting for something. That is, except for three of them. I gasped and squealed when I saw them in the center of his yard. They had been made into a small carousel, just begging for me to try it out.

"Dad, look at that!" I jabbed my finger under his nose and he followed my command as he stopped the car.

"How neat is that?" he laughed. "I guess you want to ..." I burst out the car door and raced across the lawn. Mr. Elliot hurried out to greet me.

"This is so awesome, Mr. E. May I try it?"

Mr. Elliot waved his cane in the air. "What good is a carousel without a kid on it?" He motioned for me to get on so I hopped on the horse with the moon on its neck. Mr. E pushed a button on a nearby post with his cane. My horse jolted forward as music pumped out of a machine in the center. I whooped and hollered how wonderful and awesome it was as Dad walked up beside Mr. Elliot.

"You like that horse, don't you, Liza? Its name is Down by the Water. You may come ride it any time. Just push this button. It's on a timer in case you have to hop off and go home before the ride is over."

"I love this," I declared.

"The other two horses were named His Spirit is the Wind of Aiken and History Maker." The statues slowed to a stop so I jumped off and stood beside Dad.

"Aren't you worried about the trouble this will stir up in this neighborhood, Mr. Elliot?" Dad's eyebrows were scrunched up.

"You know, Scott, you look like you could use some sweet tea. I just made some. Come inside and we'll talk about that."

"All right. Liza, run home and tell Mom I'll be home in a little bit."

"I won't make him late for supper," promised Mr. Elliot. I glanced back to see Mr. Elliot showing Dad the carved horses on his cherry cane as they crossed the lawn. I wondered if he was trying to convince Dad it had a little bit of magic in it.

I thought about that the next day when I came home from practice to see one of the statues standing in our front yard. "He delivered it just like he said," announced Dad as we pulled into the drive.

"We got one of the horses? What are we going to do with it?"

"Mom and I thought we'd let you and Tory decide what to do. Just ask me for help if you need it."

"Really? Anything?"

"Yep. Use your imagination. That statue was named Horse of a Different Color."

"I like that. And I bet I know what Tory wants to do."

Do I know my sister or what! Dad helped us transform our horse into Unicorn of a Different Color. Tory is crazy about unicorns, and now we have one in our front yard. I wondered if Hazel was stroking out over all this.

As we added the finishing touches to Different Color, I noticed Mr. and Mrs. Gregory talking to Mr. Elliot as they stood beside the carousel. They followed him to his front porch as he showed them the carvings on his cherry cane. I'm not the brightest crayon in the box, but I was beginning to see a pattern here.

Sure enough, the next day the statue named Palmetto stood proudly in the Gregory front yard. The horse wore a witch's hat and an orange and black bandana around its neck. A straw broom was propped against the side of it, and a bucket of apples sat at its front feet. Fake spider webs were draped across its body and hung down, waving in the breeze. It stood in the center of a circle of pumpkins, mums, and bales of straw. It was so cool.

I looked across the street and saw Rico Salas walking beside Mr. Elliot, looking at the cherry cane. One by one, it happened that way. A neighbor would approach Mr. Elliot to talk about the carousel and all the changes in the neighborhood. They would chat about the cherry cane, share sweet tea, and the next day a statue would appear in the front yard. Rico and Gabby turned Steed Freedom into a fountain. Andy said if anyone threw coins in it the money would go to the County Animal Shelter.

The Williams family placed Magnolia Marie in the center of a flower garden with benches and a sundial and rain gauge. The Deckers, who lived on the other side of the entrance received Dustin Hoofman and attached their mailbox to him. The Johnsons got Stonerside and put a motion sensor in him so he played music when anybody came close.

We didn't see much of Wanda Sidberry that week, but Hazel kept stomping out to the edge of her front yard and glared at the people going in and out of Mr. Elliot's house, drinking sweet tea, admiring his cherry cane, and putting one of the statues in their front yards.

It had been exactly two weeks since the statues were unloaded into Crooked Creek subdivision when I saw Hazel crossing her yard. I was riding the carousel while Mr. Elliot painted the post with the "on" button mounted on it when she invaded our fun.

"Mr. Elliot!" Hazel's eyes were wide as golf balls and her face was red. The carousel stopped but I sat still, clutching my horse's neck.

Mr. E put down his paint can and brush. "Hey, Miss Hazel. What can I do for you?"

She was so close to Mr. Elliot, I bet he could have smelled her deodorant. "You can take these ridiculous horse statues out of our subdivision and put them in a museum."

"Are they a problem?"

She pointed at me. "Just look at that. Next thing you know, children from other streets will find out about this and come down our road."

"That might happen." Mr. Elliot stepped back a little, and nodded.

"Other people might come and sit on the Williams' benches or splash the water out of the Salas' fountain."

"Hmmm."

"And Miss Louise! Just look at her silly horse. She dresses it up like one of those porch geese."

"I see." Mr. Elliot smiled.

Hazel turned to me. "And you! How's it going to go over with your parents when children run into your yard to look at that, that undignified unicorn?"

I shrugged. I thought it wise not to talk.

"We will have strangers - outsiders- coming down our street, looking at our homes. And they will laugh at us. We used to be so neat and uniform."

"And boring," I whispered.

"Hazel, please come onto the porch and have some sweet tea with me."

"What?" Hazel looked stumped. I guess she was expecting a fight.

"I make the very best sweet tea. Just come up on the porch for a few minutes and we will talk about this." He gently guided her by her arm. "Have you ever seen my cane up close? Just look, Miss Hazel, at the workmanship of the wood."

That was the last time I saw the remaining statues in Mr. Elliot's driveway. Sunday afternoon I rode my bike with Andy and almost crashed into him as we glided past Wanda's front yard. At the edge of her lawn stood the statue Patriotism parallel to the horse Regions Spirit of Aiken in Hazel's yard, with a gigantic hammock stretched between them. What was weirder yet was that Wanda and Hazel were sitting in the hammock, laughing at something they were pointing to in a magazine.

In all my eleven years I never thought I would see what I saw that day. Hazel was laughing. Wanda was having fun. And they weren't policing anybody or hollering orders through a yellow bullhorn.

Andy was shaking his head. "Will you look at that? Boy, that Mr. Elliot is amazing. How'd he do it, Liza?"

"I don't know, Andy, but I'm glad he did."

We pedaled up the hill and zipped close to Stonerside to make him play "Monster Mash."

"Maybe it was the sweet tea, Andy."

"Then he must have made Miss Hazel drink a gallon." He laughed wickedly. I joined him, remembering that Mom said Mr. Elliot had the gift of persuasion.

But I'm thinking maybe there's a little bit of magic in that cherry cane after all ...

His Spirit is the Wind of Aiken

After Dustin Hoofman: Outside Washington Center for the Performing Arts

Linda Lee Harper

A Horse in A Tuxedo and Top Hat Makes No More Sense Than a Ventriloquist On Trial For Perpetuating Fraud With His Art

Which is to say, both make sense as performers.
At the least I'm saying both demonstrate art
as aspiration, real artifice the goal whenever
one throws out his voice, the other, speed records.

His training proves the key to perfection,
so this elegant Friesian perfects his flight,
deceives stopwatches by meteoric sprints, disposes
of past, personal bests like old racing forms, right?

The world is a stage; didn't I tell you that when
I asked why I should hurry back to riding
so soon after a fall? It's a matter of placement,
you insisted; you should force fear behind what

you carry with you when you bolt, and to memorize
marks, how to accept the contrary notion that bidden,
most heats do fall to the swift, fleetest, and didn't I
repeat, words from my mouth to yours, that often

great clothes make the man, man universal
code for horse, in the best circles, usually circles
oh, say where winners congregate, all
always dashing, appropriate for occasion,

black tie and tails, although tails can be
problematic, but don't ask about the hat.
How does it stay on? you will persist,
and my answer must be, it's all in the fit:

the saddle for the rider, the rider for
the steed, the steed for the track, the track
for the day, the day for the play and if noir
hat fits, wear it, let its gravity-defying

mysteries remain as elusive as how to stride as
if hooves never touch earth, race after race,
how it is that even the devil in Faust looks heavenly
in a tux, his tail also problematic in black tie, base,

but consider notions of staging, to train, those urges to perform,
then, finale, taking a bow to let applause,
and tributes flow over you like the air that surges
into the sweet spot which precedes all finish lines:

the win, the trophy gleaming like a klieg light.

Blue Horseplay

Vicki Collins

Standing sentry at The Etherredge Center, Down by the Water hears the excited chatter of families entering his building. A playbill lands by his front hoofs; he lowers his head to read: Blue Horses, **a Play by Kathryn Schultz Miller.** His fragile legs leave solid encasement to trot inside the theater. On stage, four children share struggles, hopes and dreams. Young thespian Tracy exclaims, "My Aunt Evelyn believes horses can be blue!" Down by the Water jumps onto the stage, the spotlight shining on the silver dapples of his flanks. Actors and audience alike gasp in amazement.

Posted on the nearby signboard: **Story Hour: Children's Author Eric Carle Reads his Book,** The Artist Who Painted a Blue Horse. School children spill from the bellies of yellow buses. Down by the Water ambles inside the arena and follows the sounds of the author's voice and the children's laughter. Captured on the pages of the book are vivid drawings--a green lion, purple fox, orange elephant, polka-dotted donkey, and yes, even a blue horse! Feeling confident about his otherwise odd identity, he nickers and nuzzles the writer's shoulder affectionately. The children are delighted to see this storybook character come to life.

A huge tour bus pulls up to the curb; bold lettering painted on its sides heralds **The Bluehorses**. Three young men with long, flowing manes and Welsh accents emerge to unload guitars, violins, a harp, and mandolin. Soon, sounds of Celtic and folk rock reach the ears of Down by the Water. Unable to stand still any longer, he lifts each foot to free himself from his pedestal and canters inside the concert hall. Above an intense mixture of rock, Goth and classical tunes, equine whinnies and snorts are heard along with hoof beats matching the music's tempo.

The new signbill announces: **Artwork by German Expressionist Franz Marc.** Below the title, a lithograph labels the artist, The Blue Rider. Bolting from his concrete block, Down by the Water gallops into the gallery. Joining attendees who mill about the display, he neighs and nods approval. Drawn to a piece titled *The Tower of Blue Horses*, he feels a sense of brotherhood and quite naturally steps inside the painting. Onlookers gape at his blueblood confirmation which echoes the vertical lines of four majestic steeds.

Wrinkled by recent rain and yellowed by the sun, a newspaper wafts onto the hedge beside Down by the Water. A front-page photograph depicts the massive sculpture anchored at Denver International Airport, a beautiful blue mustang rearing into a cloud-filled sky. Inside the sportssection, he reads the legend of Lexington, a famous race horse who turned blue after eating Kentucky bluegrass grown above an ancient limestone shelf. Driven by curiosity, he contemplates seeing both of these horses first hand. Should he go west or north? Nah! He enjoys all the cultural events at The Etherredge Center, and his feet are firmly grounded in Aiken. He will forever be a USCA Pacer!

Down by the Water

Dreaming in the Garden

Malaika Favorite

Resting under the magnolia tree
not at all the horse I used to be,
a proud runner admired by all
now I may as well be this tree.

Evenings, the women in wide skirts
paraded near the reflecting pool
in Hopelands Garden while I stood
guard duty at the Whiskey Road gate.

I wish I was in Monet's garden.
I heard the ladies call me that.
Look they said it's Monet's garden
with water lilies? No, it's magnolias;

Magnolia Marie that's the one,
she ran so fast the wind had to follow

three paces behind.
That horse outran a storm.

They crowned her with magnolias
she must have eaten them.
She could go to the horse's ball
dressed like a magnolia tree, they laughed.

Who was Monet and where is his garden?
I thought this pool was a horse trough
for horses to refresh themselves after galloping
with riders bouncing on their backs.

I pranced near the reflecting pool
took a sip, and admired the water lilies
spread out like umbrellas
shading the golden fish from the sun.

I remembered how proudly I paced after the race;
people cheered, as cameras flashed in my face.
I reared my head up sniffing the perfume
drifting through the air. I slipped,

one leg twisted; I could trot proudly no more.
Now I am hitched to this platform, watching
children with cotton candy perfuming the air,
but oh the glory days, long gone.

The Protector

Mary Beth Gibson

"Tuck me in."

"Tuck you in? You've got to be kidding." It wasn't because she was my eighty-two-year-old mother that I was baffled. It was because I had never been tucked in once in my entire life. As I poked the blanket and sheet between the mattress and box spring, I chuckled, saying, "You know, I didn't really know what that meant till I saw it on TV."

"Is it too much to ask that you take care of me?" Mom mumbled. "Years and years I spent coddling you."

Coddling? Let's just say my 1950s upbringing brought to mind neither Norman Rockwell nor June Cleaver. Never was I met at the door after school with a plate of warm chocolate chip cookies. There was no snuggling on the couch, sharing a favorite book. And definitely no bed-tucking.

My mother had always been plainspoken and down-to-earth. I can count on one hand the number of times I saw a tear escape her eye. Whether I suffered a headache or heartache, her response was, "Take an aspirin. You'll be fine."

Oh, I was loved. I never doubted it. As an only child, we'd actually been close. I admired Mom for her stubborn independence, wry wit, and love of life. In many ways, I was just like her. Including that we both came from the Suck-It-Up Pamper-Free School of Nursing Sick Relatives.

All was well until a few months ago when she had a massive heart attack. Always a healthy, active woman, she now looked tiny and frail. She had hardly been sick a day in her life, but other problems rapidly followed and we returned to the hospital time and again. The ordeal had taken its toll on us both.

That very morning, I'd fixed her breakfast. Half a muffin, a fruit cup, and a small glass of orange juice. "Be sure to eat all this," I told her. "You're starving yourself."

"I don't want to eat."

"I know, Mom. But you can't get better unless you do." I went off to take my bath and dress. When I returned, the plate beside her held only a morsel of muffin and an empty fruit cup. "You ate all that?" I said. "Fantastic."

"Uh huh," she answered. "I'll take my pills now with this juice."

I took out the refill bottle of one of her many medications. Throwing the pharmacy bag away, I did a double-take. There in the trash sat the muffin and the fruit, dumped out.

My blood began to simmer. "What's this?"

"I told you I'm not hungry."

"Mom, you lied." This from the woman who'd imprinted my brain in infancy with "Better to be hurt by your honesty than pleased by your lies."

"I know." She even giggled.

"Not funny."

Later that afternoon, I was dusting "Ancestor Alley" as I liked to call the array of my forebears' portraits that lined her hallway. Mom was an avid genealogist who glowed when she relayed stories about Francis Russell, privy councillor to Queen Elizabeth I, or J. B. Pryor, trainer of Lexington, a prominent thoroughbred racehorse of the mid-nineteenth century.

"Next year when you're feeling better, let's go to England and visit Francis Russell's manor house," I said. "What's it called?"

"Shut up, Meg."

"Excuse me?" I felt like I'd been slapped.

"You heard me. Stop talking like a fool. I'm not going to England because I'm never getting better. Bring me the remote."

Who is this whiny, defeated woman? I want my real mother back. I took a deep breath. "Get it yourself. It's only a few feet away."

"Why are you harassing me?" she called out. "Anyone can see I'm weak. I worked my fingers to the bone raising you, but now that I need a little TLC, you can't bear to do the least thing."

Oh Lord. Here come the tears. Her crying game really pissed me off. I could barely tolerate her manipulations. And now this pleading to be tucked in. Last week I heard her complain to her friend on the phone that I treated her like a child. I bit my tongue and did not say what I was thinking. *Then stop acting like one.*

After the tucking, I pulled an extra blanket right up to her chin where she liked it and headed out for much-needed time to myself.

"Meg, stay with me," she whimpered. "At least till I fall asleep."

With gritted teeth, I answered, "Sure, Mom," and settled into an overstuffed chair in the corner, feet propped on the ottoman.

I'm not really sure which of us fell asleep first, but in the dead of night I snapped awake. Was I roused by that branch scratching the window or Mom mumbling in her sleep? The moon's glow illuminated her tosses and turns. Another restless night.

"Mama," she called out. "Where are you?" Her dreams lately had been so vivid that in the morning, I could barely convince her they weren't real.

A piercing shriek nearly caused me to jump out of my skin.

"Damn that branch!" As I turned to glare at the offending bough, my heart screeched to a halt. There in the tall window was some sort of apparition. With only the property's security light to go by, I saw a sky blue horse with white patches and fiery eyes. The strange creature pawed the ground and furiously wove its head back and forth. Atop him, with a tight grip on the reins, sat a severe-looking man from a former age. The weathered, elderly man peered through the pane directly at Mom.

I realized I was holding my breath, so I pulled in a lungful of air. *Whew! You're losing your mind*, I told myself, then closed my eyes and shook my head, hoping to clear it. When I next looked, the horse was tethered to a thick branch. I wheezed with near-hysteria to see a stirring on its near side like a movie of—why, a horse race!

"Oh," said a gravelly voice. *"You're* here."

Sweet Jesus! The old man from the horse now stood three or four feet from the foot of Mom's bed. His clothing was straight from the 1800s: a loose-fitting white linen shirt, wool pants, and a well-worn vest. With a floppy hat in his hand, he scowled as he scrutinized me.

I struggled to find my voice, finally blurting, "Who are you?"

He arched a disdainful brow at me. "You don't know?"

I fumbled for my cell phone. "I-I'm calling the police!"

"And tell them what? You've no idea who I am. Yet, you've been hounding me for years."

I stopped mid-dial. "Hounding?"

"Pestering, badgering, annoying. Call it what you will."

"I know you?" I asked. "How could I know you?" I wracked my brain. *Wait. The portrait in the hall* ... no, my conclusion was too outlandish to admit, but so was that horse. "Um, are you ... my ancestor? J. B. Pryor?"

"Afraid to say, ain't you? Worried you're a mite off your chump."

"Huh?"

"Out of your head," he explained. "Well, fear not. You said it right. I am he." He turned to look at my mother, still tossing and totally unaware.

I was overwhelmed, to say the least. He was my great-great-grandfather, the horse trainer of the famous Lexington. After Mom told me that in 1848, he'd married the slave daughter of his employer, I started researching him myself.

Questions swirled through my brain, but refused to come into focus, leaving me to burst out with, "How are you here? Are you a ghost?" *A figment of my imagination?* "Not that I believe in ghosts."

"You are a botheration," he barked. "I am not here to satisfy your curiosity." He sighed. "I'm a spirit; it's not the same. Tonight is a mystical time, the night the horses come alive. Always a turfman, I leapt at the opportunity." I must have looked confused. "Turfman—man who works with race horses."

"Oh."

When he looked back toward my mother's sleeping form, however, his eyes softened. "I couldn't stay away. My little girl needs me."

My gray-haired mother lay curled in a ball on her bed. She moaned, rolled over, then whimpered just a little.

"I don't understand," I said.

He frowned. "Is that another question disguised as a statement?"

I shrugged and laughed nervously. "Yeah, I guess so."

He huffed. "We ancestors see after all our descendants. We're your guardian angels. You do believe in us, I hope."

Since I was a little girl, I'd never felt alone, as though someone always watched over me. "I do," I said aloud.

"Actually, you have several. But we all have our favorites," he said, still looking over my mother like a new parent. "Our extra special ones."

"Is that allowed?"

His piercing eyes cut to me. "You're damned insulting, do you know that?" He looked toward the bed once again. "I've watched over Abigail since her birth. A beautiful baby, a lovely child, and an admirable woman."

"No one calls her Abigail. It's Abby." *And she's a pain in my—*

"Why do you call her that?"

"It's short for Abigail. A nickname."

"No, you little dolt. Not that."

Heat rose from my neck to the top of my skull. "Uh, you mean--?"

"Pain in your backside, you wanted to say." His eyes bored holes into my soul. "You don't even know her, do you?"

I felt my ire rise. "Now *you're* insulting. She's my mother. Of course I know her."

"Then you know what a timid child she is. You know she's petrified by all she's been through, that just getting out of bed in the morning is an act of daring. You know she feels alone in her distress, an orphan with no mother's lap to crawl into, no father's strong arms to protect her."

I was cut to the quick. I knew she was sharp-tongued and hard to get along with, but a fearful, lonely child? No, I didn't know that at all. But J.B. wasn't finished with me.

"Were you aware that she feels unloved and misunderstood by your eye-rolling and caustic tones?"

Caustic?

"Yes, caustic," he shot back. "She has lost so much, and now shudders at the thought of losing the respect of you, her beloved daughter."

My chest tightened and my eyes burned with shame. He moved closer to her bedside, looked down with tender eyes, and beckoned me to join him.

Sheepishly, I shuffled to her side. When I saw her small, balled-up form, I was dumbfounded. Before me was a curly-headed five-year-old version of my mother. Her sweet brow was furrowed as she sucked furiously on her tiny thumb. Then her lips trembled, and she whimpered in her little girl's voice as a tear escaped her eye. A serrated dagger ripped into my chest.

It was then I was struck by a horrific thought. I struggled to speak to the spirit of my great-great-grandfather. "Are you here to take her?" I whispered. "Please, please don't take her."

He did not answer. He merely leaned over the child and ran the back of his gnarly hand up and down her delicate cheek. "There, there, little poppet. I'm with you. I'll protect you, as I always have. Not to worry, little bird. Not to worry."

I sucked in my breath as her whimpering stopped, her forehead smoothed, and the tension in her little shoulders eased. Her breathing slowed and she became a gentle, peaceful cherub.

My ancestor straightened and I grabbed the large, veined hand that had worked such a miracle. I stared at him, unable to voice my question again.

"Not today," he said. "But soon."

"Thank you, God." I turned to the child and drew my mother's plump hand to my cheek, drinking in the scent of Ivory soap and baby powder. Laying her little fist across her chest, I pulled the blankets taut and snugly tucked her in.

A shrill neigh split the night and I turned to see the pale blue horse rear with J. B. Pryor perched on its back. My ancestor dipped his head in a nod, and they were off.

I crawled onto the bed beside her, and stroked her silky black hair. Before long, I was softly humming "Mairzy Doats," that silly song we sang together in my toddler years. I guess I sang myself to sleep.

"Meg? Meg?" my mother called in her quavering voice. When my eyes opened, she was propped on her elbow, an eighty-two year old once again.

"I must have slept really well," she said. "And I dreamt of such childish things." Her eyes danced. "I dreamt we were at Edisto Beach on the Fourth of July and my dad carried me on his shoulders everywhere we went. There I was, sitting pretty far above the crowd. It was wonderful."

"That's great, Mom," I said. I struggled to hold it together, not wanting to spoil the mood.

"And you were with me, walking beside Daddy, only an adult like you are right now. You reached up, squeezed my hand, and said, 'Don't worry. You're safe.'"

I smiled, but lost my battle with tears.

"Silly girl, it was just a dream." She wiped a tear from my cheek. "I love you so much, Meg," she said, her head cocked to one side. "And I'm blessed to have you here with me."

"I know, Mom. Me too."

Regions Spirit of Aiken

Forbidden Love

James H. Saine

You've heard the stories. Everybody who lives in Aiken has--you know, how on the night of the summer solstice, the fiberglass horses in town come to life. These stories involve some rather unusual sightings—reports from motorists, insomniacs, drunks, lovers, and other nocturnal folks. Aikenites have hotly discussed the folklore over the years, much like others have argued about the sightings of UFOs. Of course, the possibility of such a thing defies the laws of nature and just plain old common horse sense—pardon the pun. I've lived in Aiken for several years now and have never really stopped to admire any of the statues. I'm a scientist, an engineer actually, a man of reason and logic, so, of course, I didn't believe the old summer solstice fairy tales--until last June that is.

Let me back up. You see, my wife and I have several children, the youngest of whom is Roseanna, a lovely eighteen-year-old. Quite frankly, she's the apple of my eye --you know--Daddy's little princess and all that. But a big problem developed about six months ago. Roseanna fell in love (at least that's what she says).

Nothing wrong with that, you might think. Young love happens. It's actually kind of sweet. In this case, from my point of view, it wasn't very sweet at all. You see, we're (I'll say it quietly so as not to shock you) *Yankees.*

We relocated from Indiana about twenty years ago when I got a job at the Savannah River Site, a defense nuclear facility built south of Aiken in the 1950s. Johnny, Roseanna's would-be boyfriend, is the son of my archenemy. Bill's a native South Carolinian, an unreconstructed Confederate who thinks we outsiders should take our carpetbags and crawl back north of the Mason-Dixon Line. He works in the same area at the Site as I do, but before my own midsummer night's encounter, he and I weren't even on speaking terms. We'd go out of our way to avoid each other but take e-mail, telephone, and other long-range communication shots at each other. You get the picture. Johnny and Roseanna's burgeoning relationship was in the crosshairs of their fathers' feud.

One Saturday morning, Roseanna and my wife and I were at home eating breakfast together.

"Daddy, Johnny asked me to go to a movie with him tonight."

"Roseanna, I thought I made it quite clear that you were not even to call the boy, much less date him." I bit down hard on a piece of bacon.

"I didn't call him." Roseanna's face flushed. "He called me. And it's just a movie. You're being unreasonable, Daddy. Just because you and Johnny's dad don't get along is no reason for you to forbid me to see Johnny. For heaven's sake, they aren't the Capulets, and we're not the Montagues!"

"Roseanna, I don't want to talk about it anymore," I said. "The topic is closed."

Tears rolling down her pretty face, Roseanna jumped up from the table. "Then you'll be sorry." She hesitated before saying, "We'll run away together—elope!"

"Go!" I shouted. "Save me some money!"

I didn't really mean it. Roseanna *is* my princess. I love her dearly. Besides, it had already been an unusually hot summer and the tension between us wasn't the only thing sizzling.

I had forgotten what the date was. My wife had asked me if I wanted to attend that night's segment of the Summer Concert Series, a weekly Monday event in Aiken's Hopelands Gardens during the spring and summer. I checked the weather report, and when I discovered that it was going to be *only* ninety degrees, I consented to go. I don't even remember what group was performing that evening, but I do remember getting terribly bored, and about midway through the performance, I got up to walk around the gardens. I sauntered up the hill past the Dollhouse and stopped in front of the Thoroughbred Racing Hall of Fame. I was staring up into one of the huge cypress trees there when it started.

"Randy!"

I whirled around, but nobody was there. Just this big, fiberglass horse. I shrugged it off and renewed my reverie of suspended intelligent thought.

"Randy!"

This time, I knew the absolutely distinct sound of my name had come from the vicinity of the statue. I examined it closely, looking behind and all around it, for what I don't know--a hidden speaker perhaps? I hoped I would find something; otherwise,

I'd have to make an appointment with either the audiologist or the shrink--or both.

"Randall!"

"What?" I screamed, jumping backwards. It was definitely the statue.

"Randy. Yeah, I'm the one talking--the horse. You're not crazy. I'm really talking. My name is Stonerside. You got a few minutes? You look dazed."

"Hey, wouldn't you be?" I answered. "I'm in a park talking with an art project. Tell me this isn't real."

" Yeah, it's real enough. Sit down. You don't look so good."

I took his advice and sat on a nearby bench. "But—"

"Just go with it, Randy, I thought you looked like you might need a friend."

"I think I need medication," I mumbled, but he ignored that and proceeded to tell me that he had been placed there in front of the Racing Hall of Fame after "Horseplay" in 2004, and that every June 21, he and all the other fiberglass horses come to life at midnight. However, their soiree lasts only until dawn.

"Right. Look, it's only about 7:30, so how come you're talking? Seems to me you've got a few hours to go."

Stonerside had a pleasing voice. "Yeah, I know. But you see, starting about six hours before midnight, we get our voices back. At midnight, I can begin to move."

I looked at him closely now and could see that he was gray and distinguished looking (I'm not a horse person, but he somehow looked distinguished). Stonerside began to tell me his story.

"You see, Randy, I was born in the 19th century to a very distinguished line of thoroughbreds in South Carolina. I had a

Southern pedigree a mile long. The War of Northern Aggression started in 1861, and I was pressed into service and eventually became General Joe Wheeler's warhorse."

"You mean the Joe Wheeler who was a great cavalryman for the Confederacy?" I asked.

Stonerside gave me a resolute nod. "The very same, Randy. "

"Wow! The stuff you must have seen! Things really heated up for you then in 1864 when Sherman and his boys burned their way through Georgia. I recall that General Wheeler and Sherman's cavalry leader, General Kilpatrick, chased each other around for a long time."

"Sometimes he got the better of us, but most of the time, we came out on top."

I was a history buff; consequently, Stonerside's story hooked me immediately. "Yeah, I remember. In February 1865, it was the Battle of Aiken that decided the matter. Fightin' Joe set a trap along Park Avenue for old 'Kill Cavalry,' as his own troops called him. Predictably, the hothead ran right up the gut. Were you at the battle, Stonerside? Tell me about it. What really happened?"

Stonerside rolled his painted eyes. "Come on, Randy. Give me a break. Don't forget, I'm a horse. I don't know all the historical details."

"Sorry. I forgot for a moment." I shifted in place on the bench.

"I do remember how hot the fighting was, though. One of my best friends—a horse, I mean--was killed. We must have thrashed the bluecoats pretty good, because we chased them out of town about five miles."

I was so excited to be listening to the story of a Civil War veteran that I stood up and began pacing back and forth. "That makes sense. I read that Kilpatrick finally stopped at about where Montmorenci is today. Afterwards, he beat it back toward Sherman, who was scorching his way up from Savannah to Columbia. I read where the Yankees left a lot of equipment and even some horses in our area in their haste to leave," I added.

"I guess. Must have been where we rode the day after the battle. Now what I do remember, as if it were yesterday," Stonerside said, his demeanor suddenly animated, "was this filly. She was beautiful, gorgeous. When she saw me, she was smitten too. It was love at first sight. She was smaller than me--black as night, so black that when the sun shone on her coat, the color was almost blue. Anyway, we were in love. I wondered if I'd ever see her again, because our quartermaster took those horses away the next day."

"Might have taken them over to Augusta. Sherman had bypassed it," I said.

Stonerside was on a roll now. "The war didn't last much longer, and I found my way back to my home place south of Aiken. Everyone was really glad to see me; they thought I'd been killed in the war. I could see a lot of new horses had come to the farm since I'd left to fight with the graycoats. It wasn't until the following morning, however, that I saw her. I couldn't believe it. The filly! The one I'd fallen in love with after the battle in Aiken. When I began to gallop off toward the fence that separated our pastures, though, my father called me back.

"'Son,' he said. 'stay away from those horses over there. They're Northern horses and—you know--not our kind.'"

"We were forbidden to see each other. Turns out that History Maker's (that was her name) parents, who'd also been captured that day in February, had forbidden her to associate with any of us. Pretty much the same reason; we were Southerners. Not … their kind."

"Nevertheless, History Maker and I found a way, mainly at night. We spent a lot of time together galloping through the fields and woods in the dark, enjoying our stolen moments. We were so much in love.

"But it became increasingly difficult to keep our relationship a secret. After our nightly trysts were discovered, we were warned never to see each other again. As you can probably guess, we didn't intend to abide by our parents' admonitions. So we ran away together. Had a great time for about a week in what's now become Hitchcock Woods, very close to here. You know Hitchcock Woods, Randy?"

"Yes, of course. I live here too. In fact, our house backs up to the Woods. I can stand on my back deck and look across the creek at the bottom of the draw and see Whitney Drive."

"Then you know what fabulous times we had there. But our honeymoon didn't last. We were caught and returned to Pacer Stables. The punishment was severe, the worst. No, not death. That would have been better than what happened. They turned us both into statues. Perhaps you noticed."

"Seems to me they were being unreasonable," I remarked. Something twisted in my gut.

"They placed us into separate old barns. I thought I'd never see History Maker again. But then one day, some guy named Reynolds came up with the "Horseplay" idea. The owners of our stables heard about it and donated both History Maker and me to the project.

"I saw History Maker for a short while when they brought us out of the barns and gave us to the painters. But she went one way, and I went another. Seeing each other again like that was bittersweet. It was heaven to feast our eyes on one another, but the pain was intense when we were separated again."

I know it sounds crazy, but as I was staring at Stonerside, I could have sworn there were tears on his face.

"Bummer, buddy," I remarked trying to buck up the horse's spirits. "What happened next?"

"Well, we were painted, fiberglassed, put on display for a while, and then auctioned off. I really don't know what happened to all the other horses."

I had read a bit about the project when it happened, so I interrupted the horse. "Most of the thirty-one left the Aiken area, but some of the local businesses and citizens purchased horses and put them up on permanent display all over town."

"I guess that's how I ended up here in front of the Thoroughbred Racing Hall of Fame. At least I'm outside now and able to enjoy the fresh air and the beauty of Hopelands Gardens. All the visitors make things even more interesting. Kids are always touching me and asking their parents if they can sit on me, but they aren't allowed. I love kids.

"I discovered that over time, my eyesight had gotten especially sharp. One day, as I was gazing all around the Gardens, I looked across Whiskey Road at the Green Boundary Club. It's a little over a quarter of a mile away, through the trees, and over the wall. Imagine my surprise and delight to see History Maker standing on the front lawn! Whoever had purchased her at the auction had given her to the Green Boundary Club. And she saw me too. We recognized each other instantly. But, of course, we were mute, immovable statues and could do nothing but look at one another. Again, very bittersweet. So close, and yet so far."

Stonerside blinked a few times, as if he was trying to come back to himself.

I knew he had returned, though, when he asked, "Randy, you still with me? I know I've rambled on for a long time. It's probably pretty boring to you."

It wasn't, not at all, and I assured Stonerside of such. "No, Stonerside. I'm fascinated by your story. Unfortunately, it's too close to something going on in my own life right now for comfort. But listen, you really don't have it so bad. Have you heard of John Keats, the English Romantic poet?"

"Yeah, I have. General Wheeler was an avid reader as well as a real Southern gentleman, and he used to read poetry. I think Keats was one of his favorites, along with Shelley and Byron. General Wheeler was an incurable romantic himself. Even wrote a poem about me. But that's for another time. Sure, I've heard of Keats. So what got you thinking about him?"

"Well, I couldn't help thinking of one of his poems --'Ode on a Grecian Urn,' it's called. The speaker of the poem is gazing at this old urn, one with various painted scenes around it. One of the scenes depicts a young Greek fellow, and he's chasing this beautiful Greek maiden. In fact, he's reaching out, and his hand is a fraction of an inch away from actually touching her. But they're frozen in time on the urn, you see, and so they'll always be in those positions. So close, but still--reminds me of you and History Maker. You're so close to her, but you guys are frozen in your fiberglass shells--except of course one night of the year. I think Keats has a word of wisdom for you. In the poem's second stanza, he has the speaker of his poem tell the love-smitten Greek youth on the urn:

Bold lover, never, never canst thou kiss
Though winning near the goal – yet, do not grieve
She cannot fade, though thou hast not thy bliss,
For ever wilt thou love, and she be fair!

"You see, Stonerside, he tells the guy that their love, while only imaginary and spiritual, is better than if it were sensual."

The big horse's eyes lit up. "It's like a kid on Christmas Eve. But forever! I see what you mean."

For a moment, neither of us spoke, and I remember sensing the soft twilight shadows and the breeze wafting the music through the garden's loveliness.

"You've made me feel a lot better, Randy. I think History Maker and I have the best of both worlds, because once a year, we do come alive, and that night is tonight! It's June 21, and when we hear the stroke of midnight on the courthouse clock, we'll gallop off together into Hitchcock Woods for six hours together!"

I tried to feel excited for Stonerside and his filly, but the story drove home my own prejudices. I had to make things right with Roseanna.

"Roseanna, oh Roseanna … wait!"

"Randy, Randy, wake up, wake up." It was my wife, shaking me.

"What? What?" I stammered, confused and dazed.

"I've been looking all over for you. The concert ended twenty minutes ago. And you were up here. Asleep, of all things. Come on, let's go home."

My wife and I walked over to the Green Boundary Club lot across Whiskey Road where the car was parked. I looked up the hill to the front of the clubhouse and gazed for a moment at the fiberglass horse statue on the lawn. As I took in its majestic beauty, I thought about Stonerside and all he'd told me. Was that all a dream? It had seemed so real. I wanted it to be real. I wanted these two horses, who had kept love's passion alive in the face of so much bigoted resistance, to be reunited tonight— even if it were only for a few hours.

"Have a good night, History Maker," I murmured.

"What did you say, Randy?"

"Nothing, honey. Nothing at all. I was just--daydreaming, I guess."

When we returned home, I went immediately and knocked on Roseanna's bedroom door. I held my breath until the knob turned, and she looked at me with those beautiful blue eyes. She never looked so lovely to me.

"Roseanna, I love you. Can you forgive me? Come on into the den. I've got a lot of apologizing to do for the way I've treated you."

Roseanna and I sat in the den and talked for hours. Finally, I looked up at the clock on the mantel. "Wow! It's after midnight. Let's go to bed. I know you'll want to see Johnny tomorrow. I'll call his dad in the morning."

"Oh, Daddy, I love you." Roseanna gave me a peck on the cheek and then disappeared down the hall.

I knew I wouldn't be able to sleep for a while, so I went and sat on the back deck, staring into the clear night sky and gazing at the Milky Way and a billion stars. I looked out into Hitchcock Woods and thought of Robert Frost's line, "The woods are lovely, dark, and deep," when I heard the sound of horses galloping.

I smiled, as horse whinnying split the humid air.

Tales of Hoofman

Lorraine Ray

"Dustin Hoffman, one of the finest actors of our time, winner of two Academy Awards and countless others, was recently involved in a project for HBO called 'Luck,' and, unfortunately, his ran out. The series was cancelled because three of the racehorses used in this film died on the set, and actor-producer, Dustin Hoffman, was left bearing the responsibility for those lives, as well as for the failure of the series."

– www.tvguide.com

A distinguished-looking gentleman with wavy black hair and a resonant baritone voice was preparing to address the crowd of people on Laurens Street near Barnwell. Members of the media were buzzing; cameras were flashing; anticipation was mounting – it was a "big deal" on this brisk and breezy spring Tuesday in the quiet city of Aiken, South Carolina.

And there he was – Twilight Zone's own Rod Serling, right there in front of the Stoplight Deli where he was set to produce and narrate a special docudrama based on the hit series and aptly named, "The Stoplight Zone."

"Today I stand in front of a popular deli in downtown Aiken, South Carolina. Aiken is a charming southeastern town known for its friendliness, its quaint downtown, and its vibrant equestrian culture. Also known for its emphasis on 'character,' Aiken designates a particular character trait to be emphasized each month. The character trait for April is *Attentiveness*. And you all, or should I say 'y'all,' have been just that! But . . . I digress.

"In a 2003 project called 'Horseplay,' local artists created statues of horses which now appear at various locations throughout the community. Today, one of those statues, humorously named 'Dustin Hoofman,' stands in front of the Aiken Community Playhouse in his paintbrush tuxedo, complete with top hat and cane. Though performers typically look outward at their audience, surprisingly Dustin's face points to the ground, as if his luck – like that of his celebrity counterpart Dustin Hoffman – has run out.

"I'm here in Aiken to produce and tell his story. Ladies and Gentlemen, Dustin Hoofman has entered another dimension, a dimension not only of sight and sound, but of mind. It's the dimension we call *imagination*. You're moving into a land of both shadow and substance, of things and ideas. You've just crossed over into . . . 'The Stoplight Zone.'"

Back on Newberry Street where 'Hoofman' stands, there was a ruckus, as swarms of people gathered, hoping to witness a supernatural drama. Actually, something dramatic **was** happening, but no one was able to see it or perceive it.

In the boundless realm of "The Stoplight Zone," the personality of *Dustin Hoffman* took up residence in the fiberglass frame of Dustin Hoofman. Hoffman was frustrated, to say the least. Trying to keep his sense of humor, however, he offered a desperate plea on the off-chance someone would respond: "Hey, let me outta here! This is big mistake. I'm *not* a *statue*. I'm not even a horse. I'm a person and I'm seriously famous. I won two Oscars and numerous other awards. Did you see me in 'All the President's Men'? 'Kramer vs. Kramer'? 'Rain Man'? How about 'Tootsie'? 'Papillon'? Surely you remember at least one of these."

Hoofman realized no one heard him but continued his tirade, if only to vent and amuse himself. He even went so far as to speak in the vernacular of some of his best-known characters as if *that* would get someone's attention. But of course it didn't. And so he continued, with all the fervor of a stumping politician.

"Come one, come all, and hear my tale of 'whoa'! Hoofman's the name. Statue's the game. Once I was 'saddled' with responsibility; now I'm in danger of *being* saddled. Why has the universe 'reigned' on my parade? I always wanted a *stable* life, not life in a stable. *Why* am I here? Hmmm . . . maybe I should take a 'Gallop' poll. Hey, hey everybody – listen! Yeah, I've always believed 'hay' was a greeting, not an entrée."

Completely humiliated by the silence, Dustin started guffawing at his own jokes. "I know what I can do," he chortled. "Maybe I should try to 'whinny' the lottery and *buy* my way outta here. C'mon, all ye good folk of Aiken, don't be 'neigh' sayers. Yes my luck ran out – literally and figuratively.

I'm sure you heard about the HBO series I produced. I didn't mean for it to happen. Is that why I'm here? Trapped in this metal carcass with only a hat and can to remind me I'm in show business? Ladies and gentlemen, hear me out. I need *someone* in this town to come to my rescue. Good people, I'm not a person who believes in things I cannot see or prove, but I believe someone somehow will help me. And so, I say to you – whether you hear me or not – may the 'horse' be with you." And Dustin chuckled again, but this time it was a bit forced and mechanical.

The Newberry Street plaza had rarely had this many visitors, except maybe for the Lobster Races or performance at the Playhouse. All week there had been curiosity-seekers, media, couples on dates, families with children, all streaming in and out, hoping for a glimpse of something strange and mysterious, hoping to witness Dustin Hoofman's journey into "The Stoplight Zone."

So far that had not happened, but it was still morning on this seemingly ordinary Wednesday. Already tantalizing scents of baking dough, cheese, and oregano drifted out from the pizza place next door, stimulating premature hunger pangs in many of those gathered on the plaza. In fact, since Mr. Serling's arrival, the restaurant had enjoyed record-breaking sales.

People chattered and speculated about what they thought might happen to Hoofman. One such conversation went like this: "Well, I don't care what Mr. Serling says, I don't see anything happening. I think it's a big hoax."

Her male companion added, "Yeah, Hoofman looks just like he always does, a statue, completely oblivious and inattentive."

"Yeah, I totally agree. And don't forget Hoffman was in-attentive to the well-being of those horses. We in Aiken South Carolina don't take kindly to mistreatment of horses!"

With a haunting, mysterious tone, he stage-whispered, "Funny you should use the word *inattentive*. Isn't that the char-acter trait for this month? Please with his observation, he then mimicked with creepy clarity the infamous "Twilight Zone" theme song: Doo doo doo doo, doo doo doo doo . . ."

"Oh, right. Now you're getting all spooky on me."

"Maybe – and maybe not. Bwa-hahahahaha!"

"Mommy, I wanna see the horsey. I wanna *wide* him. Pwease, pwease." Tess Keplar couldn't resist seeing the san-dy-haired little Tripp excited, especially given all he'd been through lately. So she lifted her thin, fragile boy onto Dustin Hoofman's back, touched by how proud, content - and surpris-ingly natural - he looked sitting there.

Dustin, still feeling frustrated and ornery, became the rough, tough, non-nonsense *Washington Post* reporter Carl Bernstein of "All the President's Men." He even managed to sound like he had a cigarette hanging from his mouth as he barked to Tripp, "Hey kid, you pee on my back and I'll turn into a bucking bronco before you can say, 'My Friend Flicka.'"

Tripp giggled uncontrollably because this crazy horse not only talked, but he talked about "pee," a topic his mother en-couraged him to bring up only to her or his doctor. "Did you talk to me?" Tripp asked hesitantly.

"You heard me?" *Damn. He heard me.* "Kid, did you really hear me?"

"Yeah, I did," he said with exuberant delight.

"Then please tell me I'm not gonna have a puddle on my back."

"No, Silly, I haven't had accidents since I was little. I'm four now. Hey, you talk sorta funny."

Tripp's mother sat on a nearby bench, unable to hear Hoofman, aware only that her darling boy was happily chattering away to himself. Tess was one of those rare Aiken residents: She was actually *from* South Carolina, and her speech carried the flavor of good southern breeding combined with warmth and authentic femininity. Her amber eyes reflected forty years of living, significant pain, and the wisdom obtained from both, yet her youthful pigtails and slim figure belied it all.

"Giddyup, Horsey! Giddyup!" Tripp pulled out two imaginary guns. "Bang, bang, pow, pow, pow, pow. That'll teach ya, you baddie. Gonna lock you up now."

"Hey Skinny Kid, do you know I caught some really bad guys in my day? In fact, my partner and I blew apart the whole Watergate scandal."

"Huh?"

"Oh, uh, I guess that's not very exciting to a rootin'-tootin' cowboy like you. Say, Slim Jim, when you're finished shootin' up bad guys, ask your pretty mom to take you out for an ice cream sundae. You need some meat on your bones. Oh, and save me the cherry. Whaddya say?"

Shouting at the top of his lungs, Tripp yelled, "Hey Mom, after I wide the horsey can we go have some ice cweam? And I want a cheh-wee too."

Tripp grabbed Dustin's neck and hugged it tightly, clearly bonding with his newly found mate. As he gleefully bounced up and down on the horse, he continued enacting his western fantasy. "Git over here baddie, er I'll shoot ya down."

Tess hated to curtail this joy but realized they'd been there for nearly an hour. "Tripp, if we're going to go for ice cream, you'll have to come down now."

Tripp threw a heart-wrenching tantrum at having to come down, clinging tightly to Hoofman's neck. It seemed - since his dad left - any remotely friendly male became a love object for him, and the pain of leaving Hoofman was a reminder of an emptiness still longing to be filled. Unfortunately, Tim Keplar couldn't handle the trauma and the challenges associated with Tripp's illness, and he left Tess to manage everything alone.

As tender feelings began to penetrate his metal heart, Hoofman's "Carl Bernstein" began to evolve into the more compassionate "Ted Kramer." *Crap. I feel bad for the skinny dude. I wonder what's wrong with him. A kid that young shouldn't be so pale. He's a nice little kid – and could be a handsome fella too.*

"Better listen to yer mom, little man! It's time to go, but I promise you I'm not goin' anywhere." *No. Dammit. Not goin' anywhere at all.* "Oh, and don't forget the cherry." Dustin, using all the strength he could muster, turned his head toward Tripp and winked.

With a shriek of utter ecstasy, Tripp screamed, "He winked at me, Momma! Dustin Hoofman winked at me! I sawed him."

As Tripp and his mom walked off and waved, Hoofman yelled, "Hey, what's your name?"

"Tripp Jonathan Keplar. You can call me 'Tripp' or 'TJ'. I know you're Dustin Hoofman. What can I call you?"

"How 'bout 'Hoof'? And you're the *only* one who can call me that, Buddy."

"That's great, Hoof. Are you sure you'll be here when I get back?"

"Yeah, Kid. I'm not goin' anywhere." *That's an understatement. Unless I can miraculously figure out how to escape this stinky penitentiary that smells like a glue factory. Hmmm . . . maybe it's time to draw on the escape artistry of Louis Dega in "Papillon."*

Helping Tripp into the car, his mom said, "Well, hasn't this been wonderful, Mr. Tripp E. Doodledoo? She knew he got tickled when she called him silly made-up names, so she did it whenever possible. "Now let's go and have that ice cream. Actually frozen yogurt would be better from both of us. How about Veri Beri?"

"Yeah! Let's go to Vehwee Behwee, so I can get Hoof a cheh-wee."

Spooning the last of his yogurt topped with pineapple, raspberries, and kiwi, a veritable rainbow of healthful sweetness, Tripp's face lit up again and even had a slight tinge of color. This was the happiest Tess had seen him since his last treatment and there was nothing she wouldn't do to try to keep his spirits up.

"Mommy, Mommy, I know what my wish is now! My wish for the wish thing, you know, the place that sends kids to Disney."

"You mean the Make-a-Wish Foundation?"

""Yes, Mommy. I wanna *wide* Hoof . . . I wanna wide him at that pwace where da horses wace and lots o' people watch. I wanna wide for evweebody to see so they will clap. 'Cause they think little kids can only wide tiny ponies, but I can wide Hoof. I know I can!"

"That's a wonderful wish, Trippington, but Dustin is a statue. He doesn't move from his spot there by the Playhouse. But we can go there as often as you like, and you can pretend to ride him."

"Nooo! Hoof not a pwetend horse. He's weal. He's weal. He winked at me and talked to me and asked me for a cheh-wee."

It was clear Tripp was about to cry again and Tess couldn't take it. "It's gonna be all right, Buddy. Sing with me: 'Lou, Lou, Tripp-to-my-Lou, Tripp-to-my Lou, my darlin'.'" As always, the silliness amused him and perhaps prevented another round of tears.

"Mommy will do her very best to try to make your wish come true. There are many people in Aiken who raise and train horses. I'm sure if I contact the Make-a-Wish office, they'll try to find someone who will let you ride a horse that is specially trained to carry children. Where would you want to ride it?"

"At the, umm . . .you know . . . the place we dwive by when we go to the doctor."

"You mean Powderhouse Road where they have the Steeplechase?"

"Yeah, Mommy. That's it. Steepoochase! Steepoochase! But I only want to ride Hoof!" Tripp's voice began to quiver with heartbreak again. "I want Hoof, Mommy. I want Hoof."

"Well, there's nothing more we can do today. The Make-a-Wish office is closed, but I have an idea. Why don't we go take a cherry to Hoof. I'm sure he'll be glad to see you."

"I'm gonna tell Hoof all about my wish. He'll help me. I know he will!"

Hoof was delighted to see his little pal again, the only living being with whom he was able to communicate. *I gotta sweeten up a little. I think this little guy needs a friend.* And so he decided to go for the simple innocence of "Raymond" the "Rain Man."

"Tee Jay. Tripp Jonathan Keplar. Age 4. 576 Rolling Hills Lane," he said with the slow, staccato tone of the silver screen savant Raymond. "I'm defin'ly happy to see you. Uh-oh. Two hours 'til Wapner."

"Yer talking silly, Hoof. You make me laugh. What's a *wopaner*?"

"Judge Wapner. People's Court. Comes on in one hour fifty-six minutes. Can't miss Wapner."

"I wanna wide you, Hoof. I wanna wide you weal bad at the Steepoochase. Can I wide you?"

'T-R-I-P-P. Tripp. My main man. He can ride me. I'm an excellent horse."

"See, because I'm sick, I get a special wish like meeting a movie star or going to Disney. I just wanna wide you at the waces, Hoof. That's my wish."

Responding with another recitation of facts and figures, Rain Man Horse replied, "I defin'ly know Make-a-Wish. Founded 1980. Child's wish in U.S. granted every forty minutes. Current President, David Williams."

"How do you know all that stuff? You're the smartest horse ever."

"Not smart. Slow. Only number smart. Numbers in my head all the time. If I had a wish, I'd meet Wapner. Judge Wapner. I'd defin'ly meet Judge Wapner. I wanna ask Judge Wapner to let Tripp Jonathan Kepler, age 4.9 years, Aiken, South Carolina, 29803, to ride me at Steeplechase. Wapner. Steeplechase. We'll ride, TJ. We'll ride. I'm an excellent horse."

"I know we will too. I love you, Hoof. You're my best best best fwend."

Tess, comfortably curled up on the bench, prayed silently for wisdom regarding Tripp's wish.

"Tell your mom to take you to K-Mart. You go to K-Mart for riding clothes. Look super handsome, TJ. Super. Coast costs $ 67.20; helmet, $ 85.95; tall boots, $ 74.75; Six percent South Carolina sales tax, $ 13.64. Comes to $ 241.54. K-Mart."

Aiken Standard

Horseplay Playhouse Horse Upended from Storm's winds

By RACHEL JOHNSON
UPDATED: Wednesday, April 15, 2009 9:51 p.m.

Dustin Hoofman, the Aiken Horseplay figure who stands guard at the entrance to the Washington Center for the Performing Arts and Aiken Community Playhouse, became a casualty of high winds late last week. Not only was he upended, but now the beloved statue is missing. A reward of $ 500 for any information leading to his return has been posted by his private owners, who are understandably grieved over his disappearance.

It was a day even the most optimistic planners could not have hoped for. Sixty-two degrees under an azure sky, the sun gloriously spilling light on the seasonal hues of russet, gold, and orange. Flags waved proudly in the cool autumn breeze. The 2009 Fall Steeple chase had arrived at last and every facet of

Aiken society was represented, from beer-drinking, jean-wearing hootin' and hollerin' types to the beautifully coifed Woodside belles showing off vibrantly colored dresses of chintz with floppy bonnets that framed beaming complexions and cosmetically plumped features.

Despite the diversity, from a distance everyone looked the same. It was Planet of the Shades, not a bare eye to be seen. After all, who could brave the impenetrable brightness of this day with his Ray-Bans, Michael Kors, or CVS specials?

Tempting smells from spitfires, fryers, and the booths of local vendors permeated the entire area. The aroma of pastries, fried green 'maters, popcorn, and steak intermingled and became one mouth-watering call to lunch, even though it was only half past ten. And many folks responded to that sensory call, as the "cha-ching" of cash registers competed with the blaring bugles signaling the start of the program.

As Mayor Cavanaugh led everyone in the Pledge of Allegiance, a hush came over the crowd. Latecomers in top hats were still arriving by carriage. It was like the return of a bygone era. The sound of thousands singing the national anthem together was powerful and moving. Following "The Star-Spangled Banner," the mayor returned to the microphone for a special announcement: "Before today's events officially begin, we have a unique pleasure. Courtesy of the Make-a-Wish Foundation, we are proud to welcome Mr. Tripp Jonathan Keplar, age four, in his solo riding debut with his magnificent thoroughbred friend, Hoof. Tripp's riding apparel has been provided by Boots Bridles & Britches of Aiken, I'm told, special appreciation to K-Mart. Accessories for Hoof were provided by Custom Saddlery of

Aiken. And now let's given a warm Aiken welcome to Tripp Keplar and Hoof!"

As Hoof trotted gently, deliberately and majestically, all eyes were on the flaxen-ahired boy whose grin was wider than the track itself and whose eyes glowed with a joy much deeper and more substantive than is normally seen in such a small boy. If he had been a prince, he couldn't have looked more poised, more regal, more photogenic. In the background, a recording of the New York Philharmonic Orchestra playing Elgar's *Pomp and Circumstance* underscored Tripp's journey around the track. Tripp and Hoof were in perfect step with the music as if it had all been choreographed. As it "defin'ly" was.

It was a peaceful, almost idyllic Sunday morning in Aiken. The church bells at St. Mary's tolled solemnly and steadily.

Dustin Hoofman was again in front of the Playhouse in his tuxedo and top hat, with his face pointing downward. There were people in sight, but they were all parking vehicles, chattering, unbuckling car seats, or holding their Sunday coiffures in place against a pleasantly brisk wind. By their dress and actions, it seemed most were anticipating early Mass at St. Mary's or contemporary worship at St. John's. The only activity near Dustin was the fluttering of some loose pages of the *Aiken Standard*. The headline in Sunday's paper read:

STEEPLECHASE CROWD MESMERIZED BY BOY'S SOLO RIDE.

"We did it, Hoof! We did it!" Tripp cried exuberantly as he ran to Dustin Hoofman.

"Hey, my good man, we sure did! And you're looking better than I've ever seen you. Your cheeks look just like the cherry you brought me from Veri Beri the first time we met. And I saw you running from your car. I never saw you run like that! It's been only two weeks since the Steeplechase and I swear it looks like you're getting' some meat on those bones. I won't be able to call you 'Skinny Kid' anymore."

"The doctors said I'm in wee-mission now, but they don't know how long it will last."

"*That* is the best news ever, my man. Tell me more. Are you feeling stronger? How's your mom? What have you been doing? Have lots of people been talking about your Steeplechase Ride? You must be famous now."

"Yeah, everyone weelly liked it. Hey, Hoof, you're not talking in one of your funny voices today. You're just being you."

"You're right, Kid. Don't feel much like being Carl Bernstein or Ted Kramer or Rain Man these days. I'm plain old Dustin, the actor-producer turned horse." And he honked out a lively chuckle, which went completely unnoticed by Tripp.

"But can I still call you 'Hoof'? You're still my best friend, right?"

"You can always call me 'Hoof'. You're the only one who can."

Tripps' delighted grin was nothing short of a crescent moon. "I kinda miss that funny guy that remembers all the numbers though."

"Yeah, that's Raymond the Rain Man. He's a pretty special guy. Because of him, I won my . . . never mind. I'm glad you like him too."

"He's so nice and he cares about lots o' stuff, and he weelly paid attention to me." Imitating Rain Man, Tripp added, "But. now. Hoof. just. like.Wain.Man."

"Hey', that's a pretty good imitation, Buddy. Maybe you'll be an actor one day too. But wait a minute . . . Really? What did you mean when you said I was just like Rain Man."

"Well . . . um . . . you keep asking me questions and making me feel good and not talking about yourself."

"Cool. I've actually been trying to be more attentive to the concerns of others – little boys and horses in particular." He winked.

"Hoof, you're da most 'concerning' person I know! You're my best best best friend."

"Knowing you has taught me a lot, Mr. Tripp E. Dooooodledoo."

Tripp laughed with delight. "You hear my mommy say that, didn't you?"

"Yeah, I guess I did. Is it okay?"

"It's *way* okay! Hoof . . . oh, whoops, I gotta go now. There's Mommy waving me down."

"Come back soon, Little Man, and keep getting better."

But this was never to be, As Dustin Hoffman was taken back to Los Angeles as quickly as he arrived, and Dustin

Hoofman resumed his role as a lifeless, but regal, member of the Horseplay Brigade.

As had happened seven months earlier, a crowd of reporters and locals gathered in front of the Stoplight Deli. Again the crowd applauded thunderously for the compelling and always provocative Rod Serling.

"Ladies and gentlemen, this morning the city of Aiken is celebrating the mysterious and wonderful reappearance of Dustin Hoofman to his platform in front of the Washington Center for the Performing Arts on Newberry Street.

"Also, Hoofman's illustrious counterpart Dustin Hoffman, who was careless about the welfare of horses in his HBO series 'Luck' has now mastered the designated character trait of Attentiveness through an unusual experience of captivity and a profound journey into that strange, unfathomable place we call 'The Stoplight Zone.'

"Today, Hoffman is back in Los Angeles, where he is preparing to produce a brand-new series for HBO called 'Providence.' Like the previous series 'Luck,' "Providence' is about horses, but its focus will be on the unique relationships between humans and horses. The first episode, titled 'Steeplechase,' will be dedicated to the memory of one of Aiken's own, an exceptional young horseman named Tripp Jonathan Keplar, born January 15, 2004, passed away November 15, 2009."

A Latin in Aiken

Michael Hugh Lythgoe

She moved south of the Blue Ridge,
to a town of horse trails, high ground,
good footing for thoroughbreds,
a winter colony the rails reached
huffing between Charleston & Augusta:

equestrian Aiken, South Carolina aspires
to wear the Triple Crown--Aiken Trials,
polo match, Steeple Chase. From Middleburg,
Virgina, The Plains, horse trailers
bring the two-year olds to train.

In the stables, a Latina with cinnamon
skin teaches a filly to take tack,
to breeze the training track, to not be
spooked by a crowd of onlookers;
get ready to run with the gelding

from the practice gate in the flat race.
She lives near Whiskey Road, works
Wisteria Stables, rides sandy trails
to Hitchcock Woods, canters Powderhouse,
Easy Street & Two Notch. She wears
her colors on silks in spring Steeplechase.

Latina learns to live with fire ants, pines--
tall, slender, branchless boles
shedding spring's tainted gold dust
& pine straw beneath
moon shine's crescent smile.

Groom & jockey--she exercises her
latest colt--one of three Latinas
strumming mandolins at the Mass
of the Lord's Last Supper. Argentine
polo player prays to score winning

goal in the sixth chucker; Cinnamon
skin--Latina--smooth as crape myrtles,
prays no riders lose their irons in jumps.

History Maker

Marsh Tacky Dreams at Green Boundary

Michael Hugh Lythgoe

Pegasus is unbroken among stars and a blue moon.
A painted sculpture in starlight shudders into horseflesh.
Other sculptures come alive as horses without riders:
an alert horse rears at the Green Boundary Club,

History Maker follows whinnies and neighs to Grace St., crosses
Whiskey Road at the "Horse" light,
joins the Pegasus' band of other ornate horses,
surefooted on sandy ground, past Coker Springs

to Hitchcock Woods. History-making hoofbeats
survive in her Marsh Tacky heart--mare's memories
mothered in her bones: Spanish blood lines, Andalusian,
Arabian, Wild Mustang; *History Maker* is a fusion.

Clio--goddess of History--is a wrangler, a rustler.
She sees *History Maker,* sired by mighty Bucephalus,

parade with Pegasus back in antiquity's reveries
of historic steeds, conqueror, explorer, warrior.

In the New World, Columbus waded horses ashore:
Marsh Tacky's ancestors--in the West Indies.
Now our illustrated chronicler bears tales,
a shaggy mane and a dark tail. She is a survivor.

Some say her bloodlines run from De Soto's horses,
his quest from Florida up through Georgia, east across
the Westobou River, an escape in the Lowcountry.
Early Spanish captains did not survive as settlers.

Starving, sustained by horse meat, they left. Yet Marsh
Tackys lived to work cheaper than a mule for the Gullah.
She pulled plow and wagon; as a warhorse she saved
the Swamp Fox, birthed a brood of gray cavalry mounts,

hunters, plantation jumpers, racers from church steeple
to church steeple over obstacles. Marsh Tacky is a vintage dam;
she foaled colts in Time Present and Time Past, mythical,
only 14 hands high she bore saddlebags in South Carolina,

mailbags west of Missouri, bare-backed under Apaches.
Her ancestors carried cruel Conquistadores,
but the Indians treated her well. Bloodline called
Chicsaw, stolen by Seminoles, traded by Cherokee.

Gradually the sturdy little breed grew one less vertebrae,
multiplied, learned to forage in salt marsh and briars, roamed
sand dunes and barrier isles, wild as Spanish mustangs, endur-
ing, a herd restless as a mythical constellation:

The Pegasus band grazes in a sacred wood in Aiken.
Pegasus is the stallion *History Maker* loves
in the bright horse-fair-night. Cowgirl Clio corrals dreamers, a
horseflesh galaxy, remembers pastures and paddock,

how they socialize in stall and stables, their mates
from Barbados, Seville, or Santo Domingo.
The Green Boundary steed is a Civil War veteran,
part of a blended tribe old as the Yemassee riders,

as palm prints on flanks. Marsh Tacky, too, wears wings
on hoofs, flies racing silks; memories breed big hearts,
leave stories everlasting. Hear the night stampede
shooting stars, racing with ghosts, *History Maker*

is an historic breeds. In the patchy fog of dawn
Pegasus leads his band back to statuesque poses. *History
Maker* retreats to her role as a still life, immobile
portrait. Pegasus wings to rescue horses suffering from

drought. He flies over the plains and calls in the desert.
A Marsh Tacky hears equine suffering, her progeny.
She thirsts for lifesaving water holes, horse creeks,
seeps in sandy bottoms to save horses on Navajo lands.

Wedding Belle Blues

Bettie Williams

When Maggie slipped out of the dressing room, she told her mother she was only going to walk around outside for a little bit. After all, it seemed like she'd been inside for hours.

"OK, but stay close. The ceremony starts in ten minutes."

When Maggie passed her father, she told him she was only getting some fresh air. After all, the flowers were blooming in Hopelands Gardens and she needed a few minutes alone to collect her thoughts.

"OK, but be careful. Your mom'll kill you if you get dirt on that dress. It originally belonged to her mother, remember?"

When Maggie moved across the stage and down the steps without stopping, she told herself she was only taking a short stroll to calm her nerves. After all, it was only a short walk and it was normal for a bride to be anxious right before the wedding.

But when she took off her shoes and tore down the nearest pebbled path like the demons of hell were at her heels, Maggie couldn't deny the truth anymore: She was running away.

From behind the layers of tulle in her wedding veil, the carefully tended plants, trees, shrubs, and flowers on either side of the path swirled by in a barely-noticed halo of color. Reaching the end of the first trail, she took another path and then another. Maggie didn't know where she was going or what she would do once she got there. She knew only this persistent need to keep moving.

When the heavy petticoats of her voluminous wedding gown impeded her progress, she dropped her shoes and held the skirts to her chest as she ran and ran and ran some more.

The paths ended, but she didn't. Maggie raced past cypress and oak trees, hopped overgrown roots, and hurled herself through bushes and brambles. She didn't stop when rocks cut her feet. She didn't stop when her skirts snagged. She didn't stop when a low-hanging tree branch snatched the gossamer veil from her head or when her carefully arranged bun fell around her shoulders in uneven, overly hair-sprayed clumps. No, Maggie kept going, knowing she had to get away from them, from everything. Nothing was going to stop her.

Unfortunately, she didn't count on the fence.

The long, dark barrier that separated Hopelands Gardens from Whiskey Road felt like a impenetrable barrier between her and freedom. Leaning her body against it, Maggie wrapped her fingers around the bars as she rested her forehead against the warm, metal railing. She panted and tried to catch her breath as car after car zoomed by. She ached to be in the back of any one of those vehicles heading anywhere but here. But, as insane as Maggie knew she'd been to run away ten minutes before her wedding, she wasn't crazy enough to try to climb a fence as tall as this in an old wedding dress.

She spun around, slumping against the railing in defeat. Nowhere to go but here. Nothing else to do but hide and wait. Her brain raced, overrun with thoughts. *I can't face them. Not now. Not ever. They'll never understand. They'll only make me—*

She forced all that away. The panting continued. When adrenaline was finally overcome by exhaustion, Maggie slid to the ground in a meringue pile of taffeta, lace, and satin.

That's when she noticed the horse statue next to her.

It startled her at first. But once she realized it wasn't some marauding, wild animal intent on making her an afternoon snack, Maggie relaxed against the bars. The once-hoarse puffs that signaled her breathing slowed and leveled off. She glanced over at the statue again, giving it her full attention this time.

Its head sloped gracefully down, as if it were on the verge of grazing on the grass. Still, the horse managed to ogle her through one eye. It was relentless, that ogling. The statue's neck turned slightly as though it were wondering what she was doing here.

"I'm Maggie. Just ran away from my wedding. Mom's going to be furious."

The horse made no reply to this startling revelation. Maggie rolled her eyes at herself. But whether it was because she expected an answer or for talking to an inanimate object in the first place, she didn't know.

The swooshing of passing vehicles sounded behind her, and the hums of hidden insects played in front of her. But the noisiest thing around seemed to be the thoughtful silence coming from the apparently nosy horse statue. She tried to ignore it, but the damn thing refused to be ignored. It was always there in the corner of her eye, appearing to ponder her continued presence here, as though the explanation she'd given weren't enough.

With a huff, she turned to glare at it. Unrepentant, it stared back; the indentation of its mouth seemed to be curved into an expression of pity.

"It's fine. I'm fine. Or, I will be as soon as I can get out of here. I just have to hide out for a while longer until everyone leaves."

There was no response. *Of course.* This time, though, it didn't bother her. It was almost a comfort to talk without having someone trying to take over the conversation. Her eyes roved over the figure, taking in its painted coat of ivory magnolias with identical golden centers and large green leaves, all on a field as black as midnight. Four strong legs covered in matching shiny acrylic stood proudly on a metal pedestal. Maggie could see a petite plaque with writing on the base, but from her position, she couldn't tell what it said. Standing up, she brushed the worst of the dirt and grass from her gown and stepped over for a closer look.

"'Magnolia Marie,'" she read aloud. "So, that's your name, is it? It certainly suits you."

She went back to the fence and plopped back onto the grass. "Dad used to call me his little magnolia, but he stopped it when I started kindergarten because I told everyone that was my name. Magnolia. Mom put her foot down, refused to let anyone call me that. But, I liked it better than Margaret—after my grandmother. Margaret sounds like an old woman's name, doesn't it? Like Gertrude or Ethel. I've never liked it. What kind of kid wants a name like that? When I hit high school, I told everyone my name was Maggie."

She smiled to herself as she said it, remembering how daring she'd felt that day. "It was the first time I had a name that was completely mine, you know? Not a hand-me-down. Maggie is a young, take-charge kind of girl. She's fun and wild and free and all the things I wanted so desperately to be. Mom tried to pressure me out of it, but I held my ground."

Sadness and resentment welled to the surface. She swiped at tears and took a deep breath, trying to keep herself from falling apart. It was an epic battle.

"That was the last time I got my way in anything. Before I became a coward."

If there had been anywhere to run to, she'd have escaped from the sudden influx of feelings. But the only way out took her back to her family and David. *David.* She imagined how it must have been. Him, standing outside under the massive oak tree at the beribboned altar. The swell of the music as the wedding march began and then . . . nothing. Finally, the horrible, humiliating realization that the bride wasn't coming.

Panic set in. "What did I do? Oh, God! What did I just do?"

The guilt was crushing. Leaving him like that. How could she have done it? It was so wrong, so demeaning, so ... rude.

Rude?

Maggie considered that long and hard. Was that what she really meant?

Yep. Rude.

It was true. She felt guilty for leaving David at the altar because it was rude and embarrassing, not because she actually loved him and wanted to marry him. She blanched at the ramifications of that. David Emerson was perfect in every way.

What's wrong with me that I can't love a man like him?

She looked up at the horse. "My fiancé's a lawyer, Marie. David's wonderful. He's going to be a partner by the time he's thirty. He's smart, ambitious and driven. He's thoughtful and kind and organized. He plans everything. No flying by the seat of your pants with this guy." Maggie gave a half-hearted laugh that she didn't feel.

"Everybody tells me how lucky I am. We'll buy a three-bedroom house in Woodside. We'll drive matching Priuses. We'll take vacations to Hilton Head and Disney World. We'll be so happy. Everyone says so. Our kids will go to private school. We'll have three. Two boys and a girl. He wants the girl to be born last so she'll have two older brothers to protect her and spoil her rotten. Isn't that sweet that he's planned all that out? Everybody says it's sweet."

Honestly, I've always found it overly regulated, presumptuous, and creepy. But, as hers was rarely the prevailing opinion, Maggie always believed she was wrong.

Until today. After today, she couldn't ignore the truth anymore.

That last phone call with David replayed in her mind. It had happened mere minutes before she'd walked out of the changing room, before she ran away.

"You and me, babe, taking on the world. Mom can't stop crying; she's so happy. Are you happy?"

"Uh... Sure."

"We have to be at the airport by 6 am; so we'll need to leave the reception no later than 8 pm in order to get to the hotel and get some decent sleep. Can't have us droopy-eyed when we get to Jamaica, huh?"

"Right."

"Our life is going to be perfect, Margaret. So perfect."

"W-w-what?"

"I said our life will be perfect."

"No. You called me 'Margaret.' Why did you do that? I'm Maggie."

He'd sighed as though the weight of the world was on his shoulders. "Your mother and I talked about this. And she's right. This isn't high school anymore. It's time to grow up. You're twenty-three, and you're going to be Mrs. Margaret Emerson. It's a good, strong name, your grandmother's name. A name you can be proud of. Why do you have to be so selfish about this?"

At that point, Maggie had stopped talking, but he didn't. He went on to predict again how happy they'd be before he hung up. Standing in the changing room, she'd stared at the phone for a long time after the call had been disconnected. Then the mirror in front of her had reminded her of the dress she was wearing.

Margaret's dress.

The veil suddenly seemed heavier on her head.

Margaret's veil.

A new life loomed before her.

Margaret's life.

Not Maggie's, Margaret's. She had felt suffocated. Inhaling deeply, she had tried to get in as much air as possible, but it wasn't enough. The cell clattered on the floor as she scrambled towards the door, thinking she just needed to get out of this room.

Then she stopped thinking at all. She'd just run.

"And now I'm here," she said, looking over at the statue again.

It held her gaze, as though waiting to see what she would do now. The anger and pain that had fueled her trip out here was depleted, leaving her feeling empty and unsure of herself.

"What do I do now, Marie? How do I even begin to unravel the mess I've made of my life? I won't go back to who I was, but I don't know who I am either."

Neither Maggie nor the horse had any ready answers. There was only a silence so loud she felt like it was mocking her. She'd wanted nothing more than to have someone hold her and tell her it's going to be all right. Instead, all she had was the silence, a ruined wedding dress, and no answers. A hollow summer breeze wafted over her face and made the fringe of her bangs tickle her eyebrows. It was only as she batted her hair away from her face that she realized she was crying.

"Margaret!"

It was David's voice.

Her first instinct was to call out to him, but she quickly quelled it. She didn't want to talk to him. What could she say? What was there even to say? *I don't want to marry you and I never really did? I only agreed to do it because I couldn't come up with a reason not to?* How exactly did one say that? And, worse, what if he somehow managed to talk her into it anyway? She was a coward. Maggie knew she'd crumble like wet tissue under the least amount of pressure. She'd done it too many times in the past. No, she couldn't speak to him. If possible, she never wanted to talk to him again. Like a chameleon, Maggie pressed further against the fence, desperately trying to make herself indistinguishable from the metal.

No, she mentally corrected. *Not like a chameleon. Like a coward.*

"Margaret, please! Whatever it is, we can work it out. Just talk to me, sweetheart."

His desperate tone underscored the depth of his concern, but she didn't budge. She couldn't. Maggie sat there until his search moved further away and his voice trailed off. She closed her eyes and let out a sigh of relief. When she opened her eyes again, the horse was there. But, instead of finding a look of understanding or pity, the statue's face became saturated with an expression Maggie knew all too well.

Disapproval. Marie's once-friendly, dark eyes were now hard and cold and unrelenting. A wave of hurt and betrayal washed over her. The idea that this final friend, who'd offered understanding at a time when nobody else would, had ended up being like the others was too much to take. A million words of explanation rushed to Maggie's lips, but not one of them was uttered aloud. She was done having people judge her—especially inanimate horse statues in Hopelands Gardens. So, instead of spouting excuses, Maggie got angry.

"Don't you dare judge me. Who do you think you are? You're not even a real horse. What do you know about real life, about anything? All you have to do is sit here, look pretty, and pretend to eat grass. I'm the one who has to listen to them day and night telling me they know better than me and that I'm not good enough to make decisions in my own life. Let me tell you something. I'm good enough."

The continued silence offended her. She picked up a rock and hurled it at Marie. She missed by a mile, but that didn't matter. "Do you hear me, you stupid piece of fiberglass? I'm good enough. I make the decisions in my life. Nobody else. Not anymore. And if you and my mother and David don't like that, you can all go to hell!"

The last word of her speech left her mouth as the first one began to replay in her mind. Only, instead of talking to Marie, it was like someone was saying it all to Maggie. She heard—really heard—the words, the meaning, everything. Then, she was bombarded with an awareness of herself, her situation, and, best of all, the knowledge that, even if she didn't know what she was going to do with her future, she knew who she was. She's always known who she was. It was simply time to be that person and to trust her own instincts, her own opinions.

Maybe I'm not such a coward after all.

The truth of that thought was like the first good ray of sunshine after a long flood. The tears she shed this time were cleansing and, she let them flow until there were none left. Finally, when she was done, she wiped her water-logged face and got to her feet. Those first steps towards the woods she'd come from were hard, but she took them. She knew now what she needed to do, and it couldn't be done sitting in front of a fence. Maggie was excited and eager to begin.

Before she left, there was time for one last exchange with her new, stationary friend. There were so many things to be said. But the second her gaze settled again on Marie, Maggie was shocked by what she saw.

Where before had stood Marie, a proud, opinionated creature full of spirit, there was now only a molded sculpture welded to a metal box. Maggie picked her way over to the horse and ran her hands along its flanks, trying to infuse life through her fingertips. The ministrations, however, were in vain. The Marie of before was gone and only this lifeless object remained.

Before Maggie could begin to question her sanity, something else occurred to her. Maybe it wasn't Marie who had helped her with this. *Maybe it was me all along. Maybe I just needed some time alone to think, to figure things out by myself.*

"Margaret, where are you? You come out here this instant, young lady! I've had enough of this dilly-dallying."

It was her mother this time, but Maggie wasn't deterred from her charge. If anything, she was more determined than ever. So, with one last, lingering caress along Marie's stoic jawline, she hiked her skirts and tore into the woods and toward the all too familiar voice of her mother.

"Mom, I'm right here," she said, breaking through the line of trees and finding an overly made-up woman in her fifties standing on a path in a pink Chanel suit and matching pumps.

"Margaret! Thank God."

"My name is Maggie, Mom."

"You had us so worried and—what in heaven's name did you do to my mother's dress? Do you have any idea—"

Maggie idly wondered if her mother was aware of the dirt streak currently criss-crossing the pink lapel of her suit. "My name is Maggie."

"You've ruined that dress and—"

"My. Name. Is. *Maggie.*"

That stopped her already-flustered mother in her tracks. "Did you hit your head or something? Why do you keep saying that?"

"Because it's my name and it's what you're going to call me from now on. That is, if you want me to answer."

"Who do you think you are, young lady? You can't talk to me that way."

Maggie held her ground, crossing her arms across the tattered bodice of the wedding gown. "I can and I will. From now on when it comes to making decisions in my life, I'm going to speak, and you're going to listen. And, the first thing I've decided is that my name is Maggie. Say it, Mom. Say 'Maggie.'"

"What about David and the wedding?"

"I'll deal with all that after I deal with you."

"Have you considered how many guests you left waiting—"

"*I'm* waiting. I can wait here all day if need be. The wedding guests are your friends, not mine. Now, say it. Say my name."

A charged silence stood between them. Maggie stared at her mother, waiting and refusing to budge. Her mother, obviously startled at first to have her child act this way, soon matched her daughter's stare and raised her with a menacing, *I'm-your-mother-young-lady* eyebrow raise. Unimpressed by this obvious show of intimidation, Maggie crossed her arms over her chest and glared right back.

The two women continued this way for some time, each unwilling to back down. The woman in the pink suit shifted in her heels while her daughter remained impassive. Minutes or hours passed. Maggie wasn't really sure. Flies buzzed by. The wind blew the smell of magnolias over them. The creaks of small animals in the woods sounded behind them. Still, Maggie kept her gaze firmly on her mother. She'd never held her ground like this. It took everything she had to not drop her head and apologize under the heavy weight of her mother's anger and disapproval. But thoughts of Marie, the scent of the magnolias and all that she'd learned by that fence fortified her enough to hold on.

At last, when Maggie was sure they'd be out her until midnight, a loud, irritated sigh punctured the space between them.

"Maggie. There. Are you happy?"

Maggie had never seen her mother so flustered or unsure. It was terrifying and empowering all at the same time. She took a moment to enjoy her victory. It was long time coming and, if she had any say in this—and she did—it was the first of many.

"Am I happy?" she repeated with a grin. "Not yet. But, it's definitely a start."

Steed Freedom

Angie Baby

Steve Gordy

At full height,
Illuminated by the pale moonlight,
With arm outflung, behind him riding
See, the bronze horseman comes . . .

– Pushkin, The Bronze Horseman

No one knows what thoughts or yearnings may inhabit the inert material of a statue. The friendship between a fiberglass horse called Steed Freedom and a woman named Angela Metzger shows how a fire may be kindled in one of the unlikeliest places.

Angie Metzger's parents, Frank and Tess, considered their only child a divine gift. She arrived in 1956, four years after her father had moved south to work at "the bomb plant." She had no siblings. Her father was fifty-four when she was born and her mother had endured three miscarriages and the loss of an infant son before Angie arrived. The circumstances of Angie's birth gave rise to one of Frank's favorite stories. He and Tess were watching Bing Crosby sing "True Love" to Grace Kelly on the silver screen when Tess's water broke. To her parents' great relief, the little girl born a few hours later enjoyed robust physical health.

The Metzgers were Catholics in a heavily Protestant area and Frank was a senior scientist with DuPont. Church, work, and horses formed the scaffolding of their family life.

The love of horses sprouted amidst the numerous equine venues in Aiken. Family walks on Sunday afternoons passed polo fields, stables, and streets left unpaved for the passage of hooves. Angie never wanted a dog or a cat. She wanted a pony. In an imprudent moment, Frank promised her one when she turned ten.

One of fate's random cruelties thwarted fulfillment of this promise. Angie's vision showed signs of severe deterioration as early as two. By the time she reached the age of five, her Coke-bottle glasses made learning to ride impractical. Frank and Tess tried to compensate by steering Angie's interests toward other things. The little girl soon showed an interest in trains. Her parents' tales of train rides in the past were reinforced by regular rail trips to visit friends and relatives in the Northeast.

The vision problems were annoying. Angie's inability to make friends was much more worrisome. Within the first month of starting kindergarten, Angie began coming home in tears, claiming that "nobody wants to play with me." Frank and Tessa bucked up her spirits and sent her back to school with encouraging words about how "it'll only take a little time and things will get better."

The situation didn't improve. Sister Rosemary, the school principal, called one early November day. "Mrs. Metzger," she began, "young Angela is already falling behind her classmates. Can you come over and talk with us?"

Frank was on a business trip, so Tess had to go to the school by herself. The conversation in Sister Rosemary's office zeroed in on the symptoms: Angie displayed a pattern of social quirkiness, which manifested itself in her avoidance of conversations or schoolyard friendships.

Sister Grace said, "Her mind is always somewhere else."

Tess asked, "Where could she be? Is she not responding to questions?"

"No, that's not it. Her mind is literally on other things."

"She doesn't seem particularly scatterbrained at home."

"That's a safe place for her. May I give you an example of what I mean?"

"Of course."

"Two days ago, another child was telling about a train trip to visit his grandmother in Chicago. When I asked the class if anyone else had a similar story to tell, Angela stood up and started singing a song about a railroad crash."

Tess winced. "Frank often sings 'The Wreck of the Old 97' when he and Angela are out working in the garden. His father was a railroad brakeman. Trains have always been a part of Angela's life."

Sister Grace nodded. "When I asked her why she sang that song, she said it was her daddy's favorite. Then she rattled off a whole litany of rail disasters from the nineteenth century."

Tess nodded and looked down at her hands, which were folded in her lap. Before she could speak, Sister Felicity, the school's music teacher, spoke up. "There's something else that's very strange, Mrs. McElhaney. Has Angela had music lessons?"

"Not yet. We want her to learn to play the piano but she's not taken any instruction."

"She may not need lessons."

"What on earth - ?"

Sister Felicity smiled, softening the multitude of wrinkles in her face and making her gray eyes glow. "Angela has perfect pitch, even at her tender age. She can mimic with absolute fidelity any tone I sound on a pitch pipe. That's not all. Her class was in the music room listening to me talk about notes and scales. Angela was standing by the piano bench when I played 'Mary Had a Little Lamb.' When I got up, she sat down and played the entire piece perfectly. I've never seen such a talent."

That was how her parents learned about Angie's musical gifts. Tess started to observe her daughter's behavior. She noticed that, even when reading a book or watching television, the little girl's fingers were in constant motion.

Her skill was uncanny. Neither of them played the piano, but Frank was an amateur banjo picker. He and the families of his co-workers often gathered at a local swim club for cook-outs and sing-alongs. Angie soon demonstrated an ability to reproduce flawlessly on the piano many of the melodies she heard. By her tenth birthday, her repertoire included more than two hundred pieces, from Stephen Foster to Schubert, played entirely by ear.

Parental efforts to deepen her talents met with frustration. When she began piano lessons, her poor eyesight was the despair of a series of instructors. Her playing from anything printed was hesitant and error-prone. After three years, Frank and Tess threw in the towel. Although Angie was destined never to be a concert pianist, her play-by-ear ability gave her a place at high school parties she wouldn't have otherwise been invited to.

Angie's social ineptitude squelched any serious romances until her senior year. A boy named Carl began sitting with her at lunch and talking to her at recess when most of her peers ignored her. From this friendship came a case of puppy love that soon went to the dogs.

One Saturday evening while Frank and Tess were at a social function, Carl came calling. The unexpected return of her parents led to an embarrassed confrontation. Angie was left with a renewed case of social isolation. It also gave her a yearning – faded but never vanished - for something that would restore the all-too-brief intimacy she had tasted.

As Angie entered young adulthood, her parents' steadfast love – particularly her father's - became the anchor of her life. Whenever sadness or withdrawal got the upper hand, Frank's cheerful way of asking, "Angie girl, is something wrong?" always made things better. They continued their custom of Sunday walks through the equine districts. Angie displayed an attentiveness to horses lacking in most of her human friendships.

The cancer that choked out Frank's life in 1980 altered the balance in his daughter's soul. At home between hospital stays, he would lie in bed and listen to her play his favorites. "I Get a Kick Out of You" would be followed by Beethoven's *Pathétique* Sonata, which in turn gave way to "Sweet Georgia Brown" or "Beautiful Dreamer." This father-daughter bond ended on the Sunday afternoon when he breathed his last. As his anguished gasps become more infrequent, Angie's tears began to flow, but she kept on playing. He died as she played "Tara's Theme." When she finished the piece, she walked unseeing past her mother sitting by the bed, kissed his cold lips, and went back to playing. She stopped only when the undertaker arrived. Her emotional wall rose even higher.

Romance was out of the question. There were flirtatious boys at church but no deeper relationships resulted. Tess became bold enough to ask one of them what was wrong with her daughter. "There's nothing wrong with her," the young man said. "It's just that she lives in a world of her own. She only wants to talk about horses and trains."

That was in 1988. There were no suitors thereafter. The word had gotten around that "the Metzger girl's a space cadet." Angie scarcely noticed that boys no longer came to call.

Her musical talents helped to alleviate her isolation. When a need arose for a pianist for special occasions, she was always available.

Frank had invested prudently in the devastated financial markets of the Depression. A poor boy, he'd vowed that his children would never know financial hardship. By the time of his death, his net worth exceeded a half million a dollars, a sum that grew fourfold over the next two decades. Tess's brother, Matt Lenihan, an estate attorney, moved to Aiken and took over managing her investments. He alone knew his sister's net worth; it concerned Angie not at all.

Things continued in this never-changing way until 2001, when Tess's health became so precarious that she could no longer live by herself. She sold her house, putting the proceeds into a bungalow just outside the downtown area for Angie, and moved into an assisted living community. Three years later, a botched treatment that involved use of a powerful blood thinner caused uncontrollable hemorrhaging that killed her.

Angie never learned to drive. Her dwelling was five blocks from the library where she worked, and seven from church, so walking was no problem. When she needed to buy groceries, her aunt and uncle took her to a grocery store or she called a cab. This pattern fit her life like a made-to-measure glove.

During the last year of Tess's life, civic leaders hit upon the idea of a project to adorn the heart of the city. Thirty-one fiberglass statues of horses appeared at strategic locations. They remained in the public eye for several months in 2003-2004, then most left Aiken for other homes. The few that remained stood vigil at scattered locations. By the end of the new century's first decade, only tourists took note of these silent sentinels.

A statue named Steed Freedom settled into regal isolation behind a wrought-iron fence outside a law office. Angie walked past him every day. The shifting patterns of light that reflected from his eyes gave her the feeling that Steed Freedom was watching her.

It wasn't just the feeling of being watched. The statue's stalwart calm recalled her father's imperturbability. It became a part of her routine to stop long enough to stroke Steed Freedom's muzzle on her way to work. Sometimes she'd do something silly, perhaps leaving three or four sugar cubes or an apple at the horse's feet.

She'd never been much for dreaming. This changed as her friendship with the horse deepened. She began to have nocturnal visions revolving around a horse statue, her father, and Carl. In the subconscious dramas, Carl sometimes spoke with Frank Metzger's voice. The horse remained mute.

These dreams altered her routine. When she stopped to touch Steed Freedom, she began to speak a few words of greeting or solicitude. She thought she could see the statue's ears twitch when she spoke.

Angie had never lost her love of trains. After her father's death, she and Tess had indulged in rail excursions around the U.S., Canada, Mexico, Europe, and Australia. It was a mild vexation that the only reminders of Aiken's railroading past – other than the Graniteville disaster in 2005 – were the lonely whistles of occasional freight trains. This annoyance disappeared on September 18, 2010, when a re-created passenger rail station and visitor center opened at Park Avenue and Union Street. Her walking routes in town soon expanded to include the depot. These walks rekindled memories of her father and "The Wreck of the Old 97." The memories came to her at odd moments.

A few weeks after the depot opened, Angie's Uncle Matt gave a reception at the station to welcome visitors to the Fall Steeplechase. As Angie stood with her Aunt Kate at the punchbowl, a tall young banker named Tad Milward watched her from across the room.

"Who's the girl?" he asked one of his friends from the bank.

"Her name's Angie Metzger. She's a niece of Matt Lenihan."

"She looks uncomfortable."

"Let's just say she's socially limited. It's a pity."

"Why?"

"Rumor has it she's a fifty-four year-old virgin. Also, somewhat more reliable info puts her net worth at between two and three million."

"Hmmm, poor little rich girl."

"That's only part of the story. She's not in touch with reality. Her uncle has to ride herd on her investments, otherwise she'd wind up on food stamps."

Tad excused himself and went to look at a print on a nearby wall. When the strains of "Turkish Rondo" drew his attention to a small group of musicians across the room, he walked to the piano. Angie sat, apparently at ease as her fingers coaxed Mozart's hypnotic melody into life. He smiled at her. She smiled back.

She was standing across the street from the Judicial Center at twilight waiting for a "WALK" signal. As she waited, she hummed "True Love."

"Angie baby, you're quite a lady."

The voice, familiar and comforting, startled her out of her reverie. "Who's there?" She looked around in alarm. The only people nearby were a man and woman crossing the street a block away, admiring the classic Southern lines of The Willcox.

"Angie, I'm right here. Yes, baby, I said something. You know how much I love that song. Would you play it for me some time?"

Her eyes lit up. "Who is this?"

The horse's head appeared to move slightly. "I can take you back to what you've loved for a long time. You may not know that."

"What I've loved? I don't understand?"

"You've got music in your soul. It's your gift of love. Do you believe love is real?"

"Daddy loved me. Mama loved me."

"They still do. As long as your love is strong, as long as you play your music from your heart, I will bring their love back to you." Steed Freedom's mouth turned ever so slightly downward.

"What's wrong?" she asked, a frown crossing her face.

"Trust no one but me," the horse replied. "There are those who envy you your gifts and your freedom. If you trust them, they'll break your heart – or even worse."

"Why should I believe you?"

"Because you gave me life and you don't even know it."

"But you're just a statue. You're just a horse."

"Just a horse? Don't you know my love is real?"

"Why did you talk to me just now?"

"Your music gave me life. I can speak for your father. We will protect you as long as you listen to us."

"Protect me against what?"

"Danger is nearby. Jealousy is all around you."

Her lips pursed and she looked away for a minute or two. Without saying another word, she spun on her heel and hurried across Park Avenue.

Steed Freedom stood mute, with no words to express his hurt or his sense of foreboding. As night closed in, no passers-by could see his eyelids flutter with alarm. His gaze followed her until she passed out of his sight.

When Angie reached home, she sat down at the piano shoehorned into her living room. She played without a sheet of music before her, the notes a cascade of sound to blot out the memory of ominous words from a horse statue. It was almost midnight before weariness brought her improvised concert to an end. Across the street, things stirred, hiding from the moonlight.

She awakened at midmorning, the alarm from last night's unexpected conversation temporarily quelled. It was Sunday and she normally attended an early Mass. Although it was too late for that, she bathed and dressed. There was still time for her to make the eleven o'clock service. She passed the corner of Chesterfield and Park without a glance for the equine watchman behind the fence.

Several of the worshipers lived in her neighborhood. Angie strolled homeward after Mass in the midst of a clutch of widow ladies, with Tad Milward following a few steps behind. By the time she reached her doorstep, Tad alone remained from the group of walkers. As she unlocked her door, he said, "Before I go, may I tell you something?"

"What?"

"I heard you playing at the depot last week. I love to hear you play."

This unexpected compliment left her momentarily speechless. Tad leaned forward and pressed his mouth against hers, his lips slightly parted to let his tongue run over her lips. She stepped back and dashed inside. Behind her, Tad's expression was crestfallen, but only for a moment. He walked to his parked car and drove away. When he passed the corner of Chesterfield and Park, Steed Freedom's nostrils flared.

Angie locked the door behind her. She sank onto the sofa, remaining there until her breathing returned to normal. She unconsciously licked her lips, savoring the masculine taste that lingered. As she leaned back, a soft voice that seemed to come from a dozen places in the living room asked, "Angie girl, is everything okay?"

She sprang up and ran to the bedroom. She slammed the door behind and flung herself onto the fourposter bed in which her parents had once slept. She lay there paralyzed by a surge of fear and confusion, as the afternoon became sunset, twilight, finally darkness. As she drifted off to sleep, the sound of her father's voice played over and over. Sometimes the words came from her father's mouth, forced outward through ravaged lungs and parched lips. Sometimes they were the words of a young man whose wavy black hair, gray-green eyes, lanky figure and crooked smile recalled pictures of a youthful Frank Metzger. Sometimes they came from a horse that stood nearby, unmoving as a statue.

She rose the next morning, her feelings of dread banished by the bright sunlight. On her walk to work, she paused for a minute at Steed Freedom's pen, but the horse neither moved nor spoke.

This was a day when the public library customarily stayed open until nine o'clock, so it was night when she headed home. She declined a ride from one of her co-workers and made her way on foot. She didn't notice Tad's car parked behind the library.

As she drew abreast of the Judicial Center entrance, a familiar voice asked, "Are you sure it's okay to be out and about at this hour?" She shivered; Frank had used that line often to warn her about the dangers of staying out too late.

Angie turned toward the horse. "Why are you doing this? If Daddy's with you, why can't I see him?"

"I speak for him now. If your love is strong enough, I can protect you, but you must believe in me."

"Protect me against what?"

"That young man who walked you home is up to no good."

"I think he loves me."

"He may know how to use you. He doesn't know what real love is."

She glared at the statue. "You're wrong, Daddy, if it really IS you. He makes me feel like a friend."

Steed Freedom's mouth grew taut. When he spoke again, it was in a plaintive tone. "Angie, you're thirty years older than he is. He doesn't know enough about life to know how to love you. By the time you find that out, he'll already have hurt you."

"You're just jealous now that I have a life of my own. Good night." She stalked away.

In the still dry night, resinous tears seemed to well in the horse's eyes. Tad drove by a minute later but Steed Freedom didn't notice him.

The weeks progressed, autumn becoming winter. On Sundays, Angie attended the eleven o'clock Mass. Tad's presence beside her in the pew dulled her memories of their first encounter. When the winter storms brought heavier than normal snow and ice, she accepted Tad's offer of a lift to her front door. After New Year's Day, she began to invite him for lunch and an impromptu concert. One afternoon while she prepared lunch, Tad browsed through a stack of papers on the writing desk by the kitchen door. One item was a quarterly report from Uncle Matt. The bottom-line figure it contained elicited a soft whistle.

March brought a series of rainy weekends. On the penultimate Sunday of the month, Angie played for more than an hour after lunch while Tad sat on the sofa. When she sat down beside him, he leaned forward to give her a kiss and was mildly surprised that she kissed him back, lips open and tongue searching. He answered her ardor with his own.

Memories of her long-ago escapade with Carl set off an emotional wave. She rose and held out her hand and they walked together to the bedroom. It was nearly midnight when he dressed and gave her a farewell kiss.

That week, Angie had one of her occasional engagements, playing the piano for a corporate reception at the railroad station. As she walked home afterwards, she heard an equine snort as she crossed Chesterfield. She looked at Steed Freedom and her breath caught in her throat. His eyes were no longer the lifeless windows they had always been. They were backlit, as if reflecting an inner fire.

"How many warnings do you need?" the mysterious voice asked.

"Warnings? About what?"

"That boy is all wrong for you."

"No. He makes me feel right in a way no one ever did before."

Steed Freedom's head moved slowly from side to side. "He's a taker. If you make room for him in your life, he'll take over. He already has your body, but he'll take your soul if you're not careful."

"Isn't that what love is?"

"Love is give and take. You're doing all the giving. He's doing all the taking."

"You don't like it that I've taken control of my own life. Good night." She walked away, passing swiftly out of his vision.

She was less than a block away from home when she saw Tad outside her front door, sitting on the hood of his car.

She half-walked, half-skipped up to him. "Hello, stranger," she muttered.

His eyes glowed as he whispered, "Let's go inside." She took his hand and they went up the steps.

In the darkness of two o'clock, as Angie slept a dreamless sleep, Tad slunk around the house. The cottage was a monument to the love of order that Frank and Tess had instilled in their daughter. The books on her bookshelves were arranged alphabetically by title. The drainboard in the kitchen was empty, the sink and countertop scrubbed and spotless. A small notebook on her computer labeled "FINANCIAL" caught his eye. He took it to the breakfast nook where he could turn on a light without waking her. A business card in a plastic sleeve gave the office address and phone number of "Matthew Lenihan, Esq." along with the notation: "Call me with questions about your accounts. Uncle Matt." He perused the notebook's contents and replaced it on the computer stand before he returned to bed.

A week after Tad's discovery of the notebook, as Matt Lenihan closed his office for the night, he was accosted by a young woman with a baby, pleading for assistance. As he fumbled for his wallet, she slipped the office door key out of his coat pocket. The young "mother" delivered a copy of the stolen key to Tad two hours later. She dropped the original in front of the office door, where Matt picked it up, assuming he'd dropped it the previous evening.

The following weekend, two local entrepreneurs hired by Tad executed a clean break-in at Matt's office. While on the premises, they obtained copies of all of Angie's financial information, including account numbers and passwords. They handed this information to Tad, waiting in the alley behind the building then slipped into the night. The shadows along Park Avenue hid Tad's presence from passersby, but when he stepped into the halo of a street lamp, a silent witness noted his movements. When Tad drove past the Judicial Center, Steed Freedom's sinews tightened, as if preparing for a cavalry charge.

Tad's efforts to access Angie's accounts from his home computer failed because of an unexpected barrier: in addition to providing a valid email address and password, every website that he contacted demanded an answer to one security question: "What was the name of Bing Crosby's boat?" Angie had selected the question, a tribute to her parents. He cursed under his breath.

On his next evening at Angie's, he noticed that one DVD stood out among her racks of videos: an old movie, *High Society*. He asked her about it and she explained that it was one of her father's favorites. They decided to watch it together. By the time it ended, he could hardly keep from smiling.

Prudence might have dictated waiting until he was at home to try out his newly-gained knowledge of her financial secrets. But cupidity as well as curiosity can kill cats. In the heart of the night, he slipped out of bed, dressed in silence so he could make a quick escape, booted-up Angie's computer, and set about his rearrangement of her accounts.

Angie sat up in bed, jolted awake by a silent alarm that only she could hear. She rubbed her eyes and put on her glasses. Stumbling into the hall, she saw Tad sitting at her computer. "What on earth are you doing?"

He had been on the verge of breaking into her main investment account when she caught him. Panic slowed his reflexes just enough to keep him from logging off undetected. He wasted additional precious seconds fumbling for a response.

Before he could get the words out, she looked at the computer screen. The awful insight about what he was doing came in a flash. "Noooo," she screamed.

Before she could react further, his hands were around her neck. As she struggled to break free, she lurched backward, pulling both of them off balance. They tumbled to the floor. She leaped up first and fled through the front door into the night, wearing only a sleep shirt.

In the process of falling, Tad smacked his elbow against the desk. The lightning bolt of pain sent him reeling for a minute, then he dashed through the door and cranked up his car. Angie had a three-block lead by that time. Her leg muscles were in good shape from all the walking she did and she was running on pure adrenaline.

Still, she couldn't outrun his car and he caught her at the corner of Newberry and Park. Before he could resume his assault, she screamed. He slapped her twice. As he opened the car door to put her in the back seat, he heard a loud clatter in front of him.

Steed Freedom stood a few feet away. The sound of Angie's shriek had severed the bonds that held him captive. He tossed his head and his eyes shone like klieg lights. He reared, a champion ready for battle, and his front hooves came down full force on the hood.

Forgetting Angie, Tad slammed the back door shut and jumped behind the wheel before the horse could attack his car again. As he peeled away from the curb, a siren sounded behind him and flashing blue lights filled the rearview mirror. Blocked in front and behind, he made one final attempt at escape by driving across the median. This ended when he rammed a magnolia tree, which collapsed across the front half of the car. The impact stopped the car - and Tad - cold.

"Angie baby?"

The familiar voice brought her back to consciousness. She sat up and asked, "Where am I?"

"You're safe now." The horse fell silent.

"Ma'am, are you okay? What's going on here?"

She looked up into the eyes of a young Public Safety officer. After several deep breaths, she replied, "My boyfriend was trying to abduct me. I don't know how that statue got here. Maybe somebody tried to steal it."

"And did he have plans for the statue too?"

"I don't know."

The patrolman returned to his vehicle and radioed a request for an Emergency Services vehicle. When he came back, he looked at the statue and shook his head. "Whoever pulled this stunt ought to spend a couple of days shoveling up behind the horses in Hitchcock Woods with a teaspoon."

After EMS arrived and loaded Tad into the ambulance, the police officer asked Angie to accompany him to Public Safety headquarters to give a sworn statement. As she got into the police car, she gave Steed Freedom a smile and blew him a kiss.

The Aiken Scribblers

Amy Blunt

Amy Blunt, an Aiken resident of 24 years, is an avid horse person and an aspiring writer, as well as, an environmental scientist at the Savannah River Site. *Exit, Stage Left* is her first short story and combines her love of riding horses and writing about horses. Amy is currently working on a young adult trilogy based in Aiken and Montana which also features horses as the backdrop.

Will Jones

Will began writing in 2009. His poetry and short stories have been published in The *Petigru Review*. He performs spoken word on a regular basis at open mic venues such as the monthly gathering at Café Rio' Blanco, downtown Aiken (hosted by the USC-A Guild Of Poetic Intent) and Monday Night Poetry and Music, in Charleston. He has performed by invitation at venues such as Columbia County Arts in the Park and Augusta's Westobou Festival. He is a member of the South

Carolina Poetry Society, the Augusta Poetry Group, and serves on the Board of the South Carolina Writers Workshop.

Lisa Wright-Dixon

Lisa Wright-Dixon is a published writer who has been personal training at Gold's Gym for over four years. Her mission in life is to help people live longer through exercise and good nutrition, as well as have endless fun with her husband and best friend of eighteen years. She resides with her husband, Greg, and their six cats in Aiken, SC. Ms.WrightDixon is always currently working on one story or another.

Phyllis Maclay

Phyllis Maclay is a published writer of articles in COUNTRYWOMAN magazine, Lancaster (PA) newspapers,and is currently on staff with BELLA magazine. She has published children's plays and currently has her novel, *A Bone for the Dog*, a chilling story of a father trying to rescue his little girl, on sale online and locally at Booklovers Store in Aiken.

Linda Lee Harper

Linda Lee Harper received her MFA in poetry from the University of Pittsburgh, Pennsylvania. She taught there, University of Tennessee-Knoxville's Continuing Education program and at the University of South Carolina-Aiken. Her published works include: *Toward Desire* (Word Works, 1996), 1995 Washington Prize for Poetry, One Pushcart Nomination; *A Failure of Loveliness* (Nightshade Press, 1994), William and Kingman Page Award; *Cataloguing Van Gogh* (Tampa Writers' Voice, 1997), Hibiscus Award; *The Wide View* (White Eagle

Coffee Store Press, 1998), Fall Open Reading Award; *Blue Flute* (Adastra Press, 1999), two Pushcart Nominations; *Buckeye* (Anabiosis Press, 1999), 1998 Winner. She has received four Pushcart Nominations and been a Fellow at both VCAA and Yaddo. Her short story "Another Pittsburgh Bus Story" story is included in Main Street Rag's recent anthology *Aftermath: Stories of Secrets and Consequences.*

She currently is working on a collection of short stories and a third poetry collection at her home on Lake Murray, South Carolina, where she never, ever goes fishing.

Vicki Collins

Vicki Collins teaches English at the University of South Carolina Aiken where her focus is English as a Second or Other Language (ESOL). Her work has been published in KAKALAK: AN ANTHOLOGY OF CAROLINA POETS, BARBARIC YAWP, WINDHOVER, THE TEACHER'S VOICE, MOONSHINE REVIEW, and several Old Mountain Press anthologies.

Malaika Favorite

Malaika Favorite is a visual artist and writer. Poetry publication, *ILLUMINATED MANUSCRIPT*, by New Orleans Poetry Journal Press, 1991. Her poetry, fiction, and articles appear in numerous anthologies and journals, including: you say. say and Hell strung and crooked (Uphook Press), Pen International, Hurricane Blues, Drumvoices review, Uncommon Place, Xavier Review, The Maple Leaf Rag, Visions International, Louisiana Literature, Louisiana English Journal, Big Muddy, and Art Papers.

Mary Beth Gibson

Mary Beth Gibson taught middle school in Barnwell, South Carolina for over three decades. There she met and married county treasurer Wendy Gibson and raised three daughters. Now retired, she writes historical fiction for children and adults. She has been published in POCKETS magazine and won the 2012 Carrie McCray Literary Award for Novel, First Chapter. She has also been nominated for a Pushcart Prize.

James H. Saine

After graduating from the United States Military Academy in 1967, Jim Saine spent twenty-five years as an infantry officer in the Army jumping out of perfectly good airplanes, worked five years at the Savannah River Site as a training manager, and taught English and coached cross-country and track at Westminster Prep and Aiken High School for fourteen years. During his time in the Army, he earned an MA in English and American Literature at UNC-Chapel Hill and taught in the English Department at West Point for three years. He has taught litera-ture and writing as an adjunct at community and technical col-leges in North Carolina, Illinois, Virginia, and South Carolina. His short fiction, poetry, and creative non-fiction have been pub-lished in *The Petigru Review*, *The Art of Medicine in Metaphors*, and *The Christian Quarterly*. One of his stories has been nom-inated for a Pushcart Prize. He and his wife of over forty-five years reside in Aiken, South Carolina, where he teaches in the English Department at the University of South Carolina-Aiken and at Christ Central Ministries GED Program.

Lorraine Ray

Two of Lorraine Ray's plays, "Death by Lethal Frustration" and "Abe's Girls" were selected for performance at the 2004 and 2006 annual conferences of the South Carolina Writers Workshop. In addition to short plays, Lorraine has written humor pieces for BELLA, a regional women's magazine and has placed repeatedly in ByLine Magazine's humor and creative nonfiction contests. In 2005, her essay, "One Day on Oprah" was the winner of the Carrie McCray Literary Award for nonfiction. Currently, she is working on a humorous devotional which includes many quotes from small children to whom she teaches music at First Presbyterian Preschool in Aiken. When not writing or teaching, Lorraine sings with Masterworks Chorale and M'Aiken Music. She is also an associate professor emeritus at Ohio University and mother to adult son Michael of Augusta, GA.

Michael Hugh Lythgoe

Michael Hugh Lythgoe won the adult poetry contest for the Aiken 175th anniversary celebration. He and his wife, Louise, moved here from near the Manassas Battlefield Park in Virginia in 2004. He has been nominated for a Pushcart Prize. His chapbook, *Brass*, won the Kinloch Rivers contest in 2006. His full collection of poetry, *Holy Week*, is available as an e-book. Mike is a past president of the Academy for Lifelong Learning at USCA. A retired Air Force officer with an MFA from Bennington College, he is an associate editor of WINDHOVER, a literary journal.

Bettie Williams

Bettie Williams has been an author of novels, short stories, and some really bad poetry for over twenty years. She's been published in the *Petigru Review*, USCA's *Broken Ink*, and a few anthologies presented through the Maryland Writer's Association. Bettie holds bachelor's degrees in communications as well as English from USCA. When she isn't writing, Bettie enjoys obsessing over Jane Austen and William Shakespeare, beating every person she knows at Scattergories, and having debates with herself that she has no hope of winning. Bettie makes her home in North Augusta, SC and has been employed at Georgia Regents University since 2010.

Steve Gordy

Steve Gordy is an industrial trainer and training manager, retired from the Savannah River Site, who now teaches history at Piedmont Technical College. He took up writing as a serious endeavor in 2002 and has since had numerous pieces published in the *Catfish Stew* and *The Petigru Review* anthologies published by the South Carolina Writers Workshop. He is currently at work on a cycle of four novels about the age of European conflicts, from 1900 to 1989. These are an outgrowth of his studies in European history at the University of Florida and Yale University. The first of these novels will be available in the fall of 2014. You can keep up with him at his writing website, **www.stevethewriter.com**.

The child is victim to her mother's addictions
The father is desperate to rescue her
The judge treats the girl like she is
A BONE for the DOG
A gripping story

By Phyllis Maclay

Available at Booklovers Bookstore on Huntsman Drive, Aiken, SC (www.bookloversbookstore.com)
or visit **www.PhyllisMaclay.com**

Made in the USA
Columbia, SC
19 August 2019